THE ALONE
TO THE ALONE

PARTHIAN
LIBRARY OF WALES

Gwyn Thomas was born into a large and boisterous family in Porth, in the Rhondda Valley, in 1913. After a scholarship to Porth County School he went to St Edmund Hall, Oxford, where he read Spanish. Mass unemployment and widespread poverty in South Wales deepened his early radicalism. After working for the Workers' Educational Association he became a teacher, first in Cardigan, and from 1942, in Barry. In 1962 he left teaching and concentrated on writing and broadcasting. His many published works of fiction include *The Dark Philosophers* (1946); *The Alone to the Alone* (1947); *All Things Betray Thee* (1949); *The World Cannot Hear You* (1951) and *Now Lead Us Home* (1952). He also wrote several collections of short stories, six stage plays and the autobiography *A Few Selected Exits* (1968). He died in 1981.

THE ALONE
TO THE ALONE

GWYN THOMAS

LIBRARY OF WALES

Parthian
The Old Surgery
Napier Street
Cardigan
SA43 1ED
www.parthianbooks.co.uk

The Library of Wales is a Welsh Assembly Government
initiative which highlights and celebrates Wales' literary
heritage in the English language.

Published with the financial support of
the Welsh Books Council.

The Library of Wales publishing project is based at
Trinity College, Carmarthen, SA31 3EP.
www.libraryofwales.org

Series Editor: Dai Smith

First published in 1947
© The estate of Gwyn Thomas
Library of Wales edition published 2008
Foreword © Ian Rowlands 2008
All Rights Reserved

ISBN 978-1-905762-96-5

Cover design: www.theundercard.co.uk
Cover image: *Bore Sul* by John Elwyn
©Estate of John Elwyn with kind
permission of the National Museum of Wales
Typeset by logodædaly

Printed and bound by Gwasg Gomer, Llandysul, Wales

British Library Cataloguing in Publication Data

A cataloguing record for this book is available from the British
Library.

FOREWORD

In 'Dusk and the Dialectic', a chapter in *A Welsh Eye*, Gwyn Thomas' 1964 snapshot of Wales, the author chronicles the days leading up to the final event to be held at the fictitious Birchtown Institute prior to the snooker tables being sold for 'firewood rates' (to the caretakers who plan to open their own snooker hall at the other end of town) and the building shuttered to be forgotten by all bar the valley pigeons.

Taking a tour around the building, for old time's sake, Thomas as narrator enters the Sam Arnell room and comes across Charlie Barlow, an ageing voter, who is weeping into his hands. Sam Arnell, we learn, delivered his twenty-year-long thesis on Ethics, in weekly installments, in an age when the valley voters cared about such matters as principles and were prepared to sit down to contemplate them. Charlie Barlow was Sam Arnell's disciple and it was always understood that Charlie Barlow would one day inherit Sam Arnell's lectern. However, long before Sam Arnell's final lecture, the valley voters had lost their appetite for education (education instills a promise, and they had suffered the consequences of too many broken ones over the years!). As a consequence, Charlie Barlow was denied the fruit of his patience – to deliver his own twelve-part lecture upon 'The Ethos of Conflict in the South Wales valleys'.

In the sacred spirit of compassion, Thomas persuades the caretakers of the Birchtown Institute to grant Charlie Barlow his long-held ambition to deliver his series of lectures, and to do so before the For Sale signs are hung and the windows on the past boarded up. In the days leading up to Charlie Barlow's inaugural lecture, an audience of pool-playing footballers is coerced, through the strong-arm tactics of both the ex-boxing caretakers and the football team captain (who is promised a cushy job by the caretakers in their new business venture if he delivers attentive bodies), into attending the lecture.

Come the fateful night, Charlie Barlow arrives armed with his forensic research, ready to do battle with ignorance. However, Charlie Barlow is no Sam Arnell; more Evans the Death than Aneurin Bevan, within seconds there is dissent amongst the sons of voters past; a yawning boredom which eventually gives way to a Bob Bank heckling from the Terraces. Thus 'began the worst half hour of my life' Thomas wrote; the death of dignity in a community which had long since compromised such a lofty ideal. Accepting defeat, Charlie Barlow cuts short his one and only stand and slinks out of the Institute carrying, under his arm, the picture of a voter who once shook the hand of Gandhi! *Consummatum est*!

*****

Thomas is a bard in the ancient Welsh tradition; a poet who has returned from the battles and survived the war (albeit a class war in his case). A twentieth-century Aneirin (sixth-century Welsh poet and near namesake to Thomas' political Hero), he does not toady to kings, he chronicles, as Dai Smith, another Rhondda writer once wrote, with 'a wild hyperbolic wit and jabbing, numbing narrative' the lives of the common warriors (and occasionally their wives) who fought until death on the battlefield of dignity. His accounts of the fight are a testimony, *historia* in the vein of Herodotus; a testimony to those lives endured.

As such, his works are part novel, part historical document. Even at the time of the publication of his first few volumes (late 1940s, barely twenty years after the economic depression and great strikes which shaped the man himself), they were the recall of a disappeared way of life as survived by both the author and his fellow voters. Rooted deep in the personal, his works are songs from the heart. It is mostly Thomas' own voice which leads us through his narratives. We are constantly made aware of the *author* as we are of the dramatist in a Brecht play. Though the technique is alienation, the effect, is never alienating. His disgust, his celebration, his sadness and his joy directly colour our own reaction to events. In narratives delivered at times in a coruscating voice in the first person, at other times, in a more sardonic plural voice, the socialist 'we', the conscience of the Terraces, he bears witness to the communal loss.

With *The Alone to the Alone*, we are once again presented with a view of life in the Terraces through the eyes of the 'most reckless pack of sods you'll ever see', the Dark Philosophers (arguably Thomas' most enduring creation). It is a love story set at a time when love necessitated a more pragmatic approach than mere Romance. More 'love considered as a means to breeding to a man who hasn't got the means to go filling his outhouse with coal' than the 'God is' variety. Considering this, it is interesting to note the current decline in population in the Terraces, in inverse proportion to voters' ownership of central heating (and not all down to out-migration).

The dark philosophers befriend Eurona, a 'fair specimen of the woeful doctrine that spoils all dignity and negates all purpose in community'. She is the plainest of Janes, washed out and bleached by generations of poverty. For her, dignity is only a word in a foreign dictionary; self respect, a foreign country.

She falls in love with Rollo, a young bus conductor. An understandable attraction, as, even in my day, half a century after the depression, in Thomas' sardonic phrase 'marked with a plaque on the last house of the Terrace' where it all began, the men who sported the livery of Rhondda Transport were the apotheosis of chivalry. In their summer khaki uniforms with red piping, they were, conductors and drivers, knights to a man!

As a Rhondda boy who was the recipient of a Welsh language education (always a bus ride away), most of my earliest memories are of being on Rhondda buses; sleeping on a teacher's knee pulling into Porth Square after my first day at school or being enchanted by Bristol Beat – an Amazonian who, it was whispered about (very quietly), beat men up at night, yet was able to entertain us with the most delicate impressions of bird song, all the short way from Porth to Wattstown.

I recall the *frisson* of danger in each journey as we rode the doorless Routemaster type buses up and down the valley, the open road a few feet away from where we sat. Ticket collectors held the power of life and death. They stood guard, ready to pull you back by the collar as you prepared to jump (or be pushed) onto the pavement before a given stop. Charon had less power than these men!

Ironically, I share an element of Eurona's infatuation as I also fell in love, at a young age, with a girl two doors down whose father drove his red metal steed from Porth to distant Ponty. Looking back, it was the aspiring snob in me who craved the favour of the daughter of a Knight of the Valley. It was a love in vain, I could never rise to her (bus) station in life!

Likewise, Eurona is desirous of the attentions of one for whom she is a nothing. Seeing her distress at being looked through without the recognition of her palpably solid flesh, the dark philosophers seek to make something of nothing. Though Rollo is the embodiment of all they consider repugnant, 'one who reads Fascist literature and has been heard at one of the bus stops referring to socialism as a canker', they decide to aid her in her efforts to capture the object of her misplaced affection.

Though the dark philosophers themselves are above such base emotions as love, being 'too old, plain or politically conscious to be in the running for any', they recognised the needs of their fellow voters to be loved and in so doing seek beauty in what was and is, an ugly life. As a consequence, theirs is an act of compassion (not an act of charity, as charity would smack of pity and condescension, but of compassion), the most humane of reasons. 'Compassion is my country', Thomas wrote; not passion, an altogether more sticky affair, but compassion, a deeper love.

Recently, I found myself in Ysgol Gyfun Gymraeg y Cymer, the Welsh medium comprehensive school barely a stone's throw away from Thomas' old family home – the backdrop to *The Alone to the Alone*. Standing at the school gates, gazing at the houses slipping down the mountain to the river (following the tradition of all Cymer graves to the sea), I was not sure of the exact location of Thomas' childhood home. I asked the school janitor, who had been cleaning the school's corridors long before it was turned from a school into an *ysgol*, did he know of Gwyn Thomas and where he had once lived. He had no idea and had never heard of him. 'A genius,' I said. 'A Cymer man?' he queried, and shook his head as most modern-day Cymer men and women would probably do.

If the Terraces now fail to recognise Thomas completely (I was eventually to find 196 Cymer High Street bearing the plaque of his deserved fame), were he still alive today, would Thomas recognise his beloved Terraces? In particular, I wondered what Thomas would have made of a Welsh medium school on his patch. Thomas wrote, in late life, that Welsh language education 'would do nothing but mischief in minds already plagued by every neurosis that comes with insecurity'. Times can narrow as well as expand hopes. Thomas was very much a man of his own testing and challenging time. But times change, and one could argue that through devolution and the renegotiation of the concept of Welshness (in whatever tongue – let us not reduce the argument to a bilingual one), our nation will finally shrug off its insecurity, and the compassion which Thomas championed will, at last, triumph here in the Terraces and Meadow Prospects of *Cymru*. There is no doubt that Thomas would still espouse the same ideals of common decency if he were alive today that he championed in his lifetime, and would not countenance pushing compassion to the margins of society.

As a man of his time, poverty ate into him, body and soul. The iniquity of the first half of the twentieth century shaped him. Marx wrote that 'It is the consciousness of men that determines their existence, but, on the contrary, their social existence determines their consciousness'. Easy to conclude that it was economic hardship that formed the consciousness of the young Thomas and, in so doing, lay at the root of his literary achievement. However, I side more with a near contemporary of Thomas, Raymond Williams, who countered the orthodoxy with: 'Even if the economic element is determining, it determines a whole way of life, and it is to this, rather than the economic system above, that the literature has to be related'. Life is more than economics: as compassion is more than a red flag. It is a universal banner of many colours; an humanity voiced in many tongues – including Welsh! Thomas once wrote of his older friend, Huw Menai, Rhondda's Anarcho-Syndicalist English-language poet (originally from North Wales) that he 'would never have accepted a view of life that dropped down dead at Chepstow'. What would both Huw Menai and Thomas have made of a life that dropped dead at Chepstow if journeying from the westerly direction?

Regardless of any such conjecture about the passing historical moment or the changing cultural moods that make the social weather, Thomas was a chronicler who held firm, in his own lifetime, to the universal banner of compassion and it is for that reason that we should treasure him and so reprint this volume in the Library of Wales Series. He is a moment of our history, a key moment that continues to shape our lives, and if we know not our past, how can we place the present in context and shape a better future?

In Birchtown Institute, Thomas suffered the worst half hour of his life watching his way of life (our legacy) die before his eyes. Through Thomas' work we see the Terraces die and die again. His oeuvre is one long half an hour of aching loss, one recorded so that we may remember. As such, *The Alone to the Alone* is a warning that we should be vigilant, for that which betrays is already within us! We are easily sated with satellite dishes, Vauxhall Novas and the Rollos of this life; all the bastard offspring of the 'woeful doctrine that spoils all dignity and negates all purpose'. Blinded by the need to acquire 'things', we forget the one thing we truly need. Poor Eurona, denied dignity, desperate for love, aching to be, we are her. Thankfully, we have Gwyn Thomas to remind us from whence we came, what we are and, if the dark philosophers had their way, what we should strive to be... compassionate.

Ian Rowlands

THE ALONE
TO THE ALONE

In the Terraces, we never opposed love. The way we viewed this question was that love must be pretty deeply rooted to have gone on for so long. One would have to be very deep to tinker with so deep a root, deeper than we were. Also, love passes on the time. That is a prime feature in any place where there is a scarcity of work for the local men and women to do, a state which prevailed on a high plane indeed during the dark years now being spoken of. Also, love, properly used, keeps people warm. That is a fact of some importance when coal has to be considered as part of the groceries. Also, love possessing the power of making its subjects see things in a clearer light, creates a desire for beauty. This was interesting to us because if there was one thing the Terraces lacked more than any other it was that very beauty.

Our group which met nightly on the wall at the bottom of our backyard was agreed that never had so little beauty been compressed into so large a space as we saw in the Terraces. It was a clumsy bit of packing altogether. We took this in our solemn way to mean that when men consent to endure for too long the sadness of poverty and decline, beauty sees no point in staying, bows its head and goes. There was much poverty in the Terraces, nearly as much as air, weather or life. It achieved a variety of flavours and shapes that did credit to our originality and patience. Beneath its layers beauty lay in a mess and, no doubt, very dead. Men like artists who gallop after beauty should make a new set of divining rods, find out where hell is and put poverty in. Then beauty, rising like a rainbow from man's new dreams, would be pervasive as the mist of pettiness among us now and would come galloping after them for a change.

Among us, in the Terraces, love sometimes broke out. Love, making people see things in a clearer light, had a depressing effect. The Terraces, seen in a dim light that softened the curves, could give a man a bellyache that nothing short of a hot water bottle atop the belly could ease. Therefore, to see the Terraces in any hard, revelatory light such as would be given off by a kerosene flare or passion, would make the lover wish for the very opposite of the Terraces. That opposite would be beauty. So beneath the dark waters of the stream along whose banks we lived, pinched, scraped and pondered, there would sometimes flash the forms of beauty desired and we got much joy from watching these flashing, brief, uncatchable forms. They were the promise of life in a community that had come as near to a general stoppage of living as any community can come without staging a mass execution.

'But the most important thing about love, though,' said my friend Walter, 'is that it keeps people warm. That's more important even than love considered as a means to breeding to a man who hasn't got the means to go filling his outhouse with coal. To that man, anything that puts him in a position not to care about the state of his outhouse is a very big thing. That's a bigger thing even than man's having been descended from the apes.'

And, with the exception of my friend Ben, who had seen a chimpanzee in Bostock's menagerie and who thought that it was a very great achievement to have worked one's way up from being just an ape, we were all pretty much of this love-is-warmth school of thought for which my friend Walter always took up the tongs. We thought this the more interesting because we ourselves were too old, plain or politically conscious to be in the running for any love that might be knocking about. My friend Walter was a very cold subject except about the brain where he always had a spout of deep ideas that kept his skull warm. My friend Ben was married. My friend Arthur had some stomach trouble that seemed to him to be a fair summing up of all that was wrong with the world, and the viewpoint of my friend Arthur was pretty dark on most topics. There was nothing particularly wrong with me. My stomach was in order. I was single. But women, to me, never seemed to be more than just me all over again. A bit quicker to become mothers, I being a man, and a bit slower to use the vote, but with no more difference than that. We shared the floor space of a zoo and kept the

3

place as tidy as we could during our journey through it. I could never look upon women with the zeal that came so easily to the bulk of my fellow-voters.

This did not prevent us from taking a keen interest in those of our neighbours who were visited by love. Sometimes, the love worked out all wrongly and made a mess of these neighbours, such a mess as caused my friend Walter to say that if men wanted to weep as much as they had good reason to, they would have to carry a ten-gallon reserve tear tank strapped to their back to be brought into play for special sessions of this weeping business. Sometimes it would make these neighbours slightly dafter than they had been, and this meant that we would be a bit busier than ever going around explaining to these neighbours whose minds had been laid waste in patches by passion, such facts as the rising cost of living and the weaknesses of a competitive society which we thought should rank as high in the consideration of these neighbours as the itch for union of bodies in love. Or, love would leave them as it found them, which did not say much for them or for the brand of love they went in for. Or it would set them alight and the warmth from their burning would be very pleasant to such sad and continually frozen types as ourselves.

Near us, lived a family called Morris. The father, Morris, was a thin, grey man about forty-five years of age according to what he told us, but we would have believed him as well if he had made out to be older than the mountainside we lived on. The greyness of this Morris gave him the look of great age. He was not just grey about the head. He was sort of grey all over as if he had been dipped into a paint of that colour for a tableau or sketch of the old folks at home getting to look steadily older with being at home for so long. It was this greyness that made him look older than anybody we had ever seen. Even his suit had turned grey after being some other colour for many years, while our suits mostly turned green or inside out when they got old. This shows how greyness seemed to follow this Morris about as if it were a dog.

And when we say that this man looked older than anybody we had ever seen, this is not said loosely. We have a great respect for people who show the world what a worrying plague it is by looking much older than they are. The Terraces produced a crop of people like that. We have seen dozens of them who looked about a hundred years older even than those Turks who live on sour milk and carry the thing to an extreme by getting married again, most likely to some naturally sour cow, at a hundred and fifty. In our part of the Terraces, where the streets were so steep that not even Social Welfare workers who were ex-University athletes could stand the climb, we had seen new born babies wearing the very wise, worn look you usually see on the face of a man who had just called back to the house after a five-year walk in search of security. That came from having so little to live for on a hill that took so long to climb up. Too rich for the blood. Only gods should live on hills...

But this Morris must have been under sixty-five. We knew that because at sixty-five one is thrown off the Unemployment Insurance and stored in the Old Age department. One of the biggest facts about this Morris, next to his being grey from head to foot and even lower down than that if he could get his foot there, was that he was still on the Insurance. He had been unemployed longer than anybody else in our street and that made him a kind of Dean to whom we referred with some respect in our talk. He had beaten even us to it by about four years and that is a considerable feat when you think that we were practically founder members of the Ministry of Labour. Some said that Morris had never worked at all after the last war when he had won a coloured ribbon, fast on its way to becoming just one colour, grey, pinned to the lapel of his coat as much to keep the coat on him as the ribbon on the coat. Others said that when Morris had marched back from the last war, the only new, shiny place in the town that he could see was the Labour Exchange, so naturally, never having been very subtle in his ways of thinking, he concluded that this new, shiny place must be the place where they were laying in stocks of that democracy he had been keeping the world safe for. So he walked in, signed up and made himself at home, as much as you can be at home in a place with so many pens and forms and clerks and notices threatening you with gaol for misleading the Government about your work, wealth and happiness. Morris had hung on there and had never given the Government any reason to put him in gaol, being always strictly truthful and always looking as if the Government had already kept him in gaol for too long as it was.

Morris had had many children. His wife was a silent, emotionless woman, once the owner of a nice, mourning, contralto voice, given up when life with Morris got so dull it went beyond mourning for. Between her and Morris there seemed to exist no bond save those of food and whatever kind of love it was that twitched those many children into life. Indeed, Morris could be used as one of the best examples you could light on of love being used simply as a means of heating oneself. In the eyes of Morris not even a lynx paid by the Council's Ways and Means Committee to unearth such things, could have discovered any desire for love conceived as a path to the desire for beauty. Morris was so obviously a graveyard of desires that had died soon after birth, one expected to see printed memorial verses on his brow.

All his children were daughters. This was another grey feature in the character of Morris. Daughters were not looked on with favour in the Terraces. Girls could never earn much more than their keep if you wished to keep them any better than a goat. Nor was there any chance at all of a parent making a quick profit on them, as one might do, for instance, with a son who took a hand at rifling the local gas meters or bringing home the Sunday vegetables from a stall in the market without consulting anybody but the vegetables; unless, of course, the girl was born with beauty in her face and was chosen as May Day Queen and got fancied by a business man who would pat her at so much a pat. Morris was very sad about all these daughters and had no great opinion of his wife for having produced such a string of them. My friend Ben, who had spent part of one winter in a biology class at the Library and Institute, which was a large square building on the corner of the third Terrace and full of books and interesting characters, told us that Morris kept on having these many daughters because there was something wrong with his genes. You could not see these genes, but there was something wrong with them. They were recessive, said Ben, went backwards. No one of us knew exactly what Ben was driving at with this talk of genes that were recessive and went backwards. But we listened to his theory with all earnestness, for we were always grateful to have the light of science thrown on our many problems, even when the light came to us through so eccentric an index as Ben who spent too much time, as we saw it, arguing in a violent way with the lecturer at the Library and Institute about life in general ever to get a really straight line on any theories about things in particular. Ben had often been thrown clean out of the Library and Institute for this violence in debate. But we were willing to admit that he might be right about Morris' genes, wherever they were. You could see, by just one look at Morris, that he was probably top-heavy with these recessive genes. All the same, the simpler way some of us had of looking at this daughter question was that Morris kept on having daughters because he was short of coal and could not lie still at night for any great length of time without starting to feel the frost in a severe way.

Three of the Morris girls had already drifted out of the Terraces into the houses of various well-to-do people around about, as domestic workers. Well-to-do people were a vanishing tribe in our valley but there were still a few left with enough grip on the community to keep the past alive by taking in domestic help. Morris often passed on to us some of the things he heard from these daughters about the activities of the well-to-do, and the only moral we could draw from these tales, short of the general moral that the Morris girls were lucky to have such an attentive father, was that the well-to-do had even less to do than we did and had a lot more reason for doing it; also, they seemed to have a lot more of everything than we had, except sense. Morris thought highly of the well-to-do, spoke like a poet, one of the dead poets, in praise of the few bob weekly his daughters got from them and craved just such for his remaining daughters. He told us, too, that if we fellows knew as much about the well-to-do as he knew, we would have a better outlook on life altogether. We would realise that there was something in life worth striving for and would stop going around with faces like coffin lids and taking the name of the well-to-do in vain and thus spreading a lot of discontent among the voters. We told him his wits must be going grey, too.

The only Morris daughter we knew much about was Eurona. She was the oldest of those who remained at home, about seventeen years of age. She helped her mother clean the house and look after the younger children who created the need for a lot of cleaning. It was my friend Walter who first noticed that Eurona had beauty of a kind. And, indeed, when we gave her a second look, she turned out to be most pretty. Even my friend Arthur turned the tables on his stomach for long enough to admit that there was something nice to look at in Eurona. She was very dark and had a face that was full of deep, struggling dreams. Of course, anyone who took life more on the surface and stared at it for shorter lengths of time than my friend

Walter would have passed Eurona by as being no more than one of those scarecrows who flock about the Terraces in such numbers. We have not seen a living crow in these parts for the last five years.

Eurona, to the normal passer-by, would have been straightaway classed as plain, slatternly and not worth a second look, unless the look were directed at the distinct white patch around her jaws that indicated, we supposed, underfeeding. We supposed that because there was no other fact in Eurona's life as big as that one of underfeeding or important enough in its own right for her to want to go around carrying it like a banner on her jaws. She looked, as far as her clothes went, as though she had been pulled through brambles and then pushed through a thin tube. Her parents who never seemed to have given a single thought to the way she looked, might, possibly, for all they seemed to mind, have arranged for the brambles and tube to be brought into action. It was no fault of theirs. The fact was that there was nothing the parents could have done about it even if they had written a whole book on the thoughts they had had about the way Eurona was dressed. There was one main task in the Terraces. That was to keep alive. The clothes you did it in counted for little, so little we would have been grateful to any person who took the matter in hand and appeared in his raw skin.

Eurona, in fact, was worse dressed than her sisters. They were still at school and eligible to receive old clothes that were being distributed by some group who believed that we could never go forward to the New Age while we still had school kids walking around looking so shabby they were afraid to look in the mirror. So this New Age Group handed out big bundles of old clothes and mirrors and jacked up self-respect among the smaller children at a great speed. Eurona got none of these gifts. The New Age Group had probably taken a long look at Eurona and come to the conclusion that the New Age would start off by looking a lot too old and rough if they began admitting such haggledy-raggedy types as Eurona. At least, that was the way in which we interpreted the policy of this group. We will say that we were not very clear at all about what this group was supposed to be aiming at. We could not see what old clothes had to do with New Ages and, in any case, we noticed that all the foremost members of this New Age Group that committed all this charity were people who always got very hot and angry when we poorer voters in the Terraces began to march about the streets and raise a clamour in an effort to get a slice of New Age on our own account.

We saw a lot of Eurona. In the evenings, she hung about the Terraces, never going down into the main streets of the town at the bed of the valley, as most girls of her age had the habit of doing, in pursuit of change, love, films, big shops, or whatever else it was that might take their fancy. Her younger sisters snatched all the pennies that might be going for trips to the pictures, and the clothes she wore were not the sort that a girl halfway to womanhood likes to be seen walking about in in a main street. She did no reading. She had not been able to read too fast even when she was at school being urged to it by teachers. There were no books in the house she lived in that she could have practised on. Morris had views about books. These views arose mainly from the fact that Morris had a lot of mice in his house and had never been able to afford the bit of extra cheese he would have needed to bait a mouse trap or the energy to sit up at nights to choke them one by one. So, he said, he was not going to keep books about the place to be the means of feeding mice without feeding himself, unless of course, he adopted the line of getting in a large supply of literature, allowing the mice to feed at will and then starting in himself on a diet of fed mice. So, Eurona had not learned to read any faster since she had left the Council school and was not likely to until her father traded in his old brain in part payment for a new one of the bright, shiny and non-rusting kind. But she was a girl that wanted to know things, many things. There was a lot of curiosity in those dreams that lay in her face.

She often came and sat on the wall where we men did our talking, and listened thirstily to the many and long discussions we had, big-eyed, as if her life depended on the clapping of our tongues. Sometimes, she would ask questions. These questions would mostly be on such subjects as boys and love which are close to the heart of any girl. She often got us on the run with these questions for we were not strong on those subjects and our replies were often hasty and mumbled. And sometimes, after one of these sessions of talk on love and boys, Eurona would get up and walk away from us with a very dissatisfied expression on her face, as if she had the impression that we were just a bunch of chaps who liked to look and talk wise without being so. That pricked us, for we were proud of the little stocks of wisdom that life had battered into us with its bare knuckles. But we did a lot better on such topics as the right to work, real wages, imperialism and religion, and all Eurona could do when we got properly launched on this cycle was sit and listen. Such topics were a mystery to her because all she could have heard in the way of steady talk in her house was Morris trying to get an understanding with the mice or demanding a fresh kid whenever the cold began to worry him. Whereas we were prophets of a sort whenever the discussion was about things of which experience and book-reading had taught us much, particularly in discussions about the Slump. We were the oldest sons, so to speak, of that same Slump and we hated our parent with the kind of feeling from which poetry is made and on that topic we could always work up a high note that left Isaiah standing. Eurona listened attentively and from odd things she let out now and then we gathered that there could not have been many girls of her age, weight and constitution who knew more about the Industrial Revolution and the inevitable breakdown of the profit motive and the question of Jonah and the whale than she learned from us.

Morris got annoyed about this and came over to complain to us one night when there was a heavy grey mist hanging about the Terraces. When he started his complaint we thought first of all, hearing a voice and seeing no one, that thin times and overthinking had driven us to hearing spirit voices and for a minute we were upset by this thought because it is no joke to be born in a place that ought to be burned, like the Terraces, and then have the feeling that you are going to be burned, like Joan of Arc who also heard spirit voices. But it was only Morris, harmonising with the grey mist, and short of death, nothing could have blotted him out more efficiently. What chance, he asked in a shaking voice as soon as he had made himself visible, what chance did we think his Eurona would ever have of becoming a domestic worker in the homes of the ruling and contented classes if we, with our talk, went turning her into a Bolshevik.

'Peace, brother Morris,' said my friend Walter to him in a gentle tone. 'If Eurona takes in a few more pounds of the doctrine as set forth by us, she might not even be a domestic.'

It would have taken Morris a whole year free from care, cold and breeding to have grasped any part of the meaning of that statement, so he walked off into the mist saying that he hoped so, which was what he always said in answer to whatever anyone told him. Morris was as short of answers as he was of questions. He was pretty short all round.

'You just look at that kid Eurona's face when we are talking,' went on my friend Walter when we were alone again. 'It shines. Not that she understands in the bulk all we say. She doesn't need to because some of the stuff we say is pure nonsense and we only say it because the kind of silence you get around these parts is pure lead and presses the redness from the blood. Her face shines because we are a bit of a miracle to her. After Morris, anybody is likely to look like a miracle to Morris' kids. But she sees us, sitting here on this wall, in cold and heat, talking of the world we live in. That, to Eurona, must be a very marvellous thing because this is a very hard wall and

14

it gets very cold on these hillsides. So, if she sees her neighbours performing marvels like that it must give her the notion that even further marvels might take place in the world which will cause the world to change for the better. That makes her face shine. She looks on the change as something that will affect her personally and why not? If ever we make a fresh start, it will be for the sake of kids like Eurona and not for the sake of throwing up half a dozen good talkers for the history books to write about. That kid has been denied all beauty, all confidence in herself and yet she'll feel exactly the same kind of passion as the lily-skinned dames who get themselves trimmed and trained and lacquered from the cradle up for the one purpose of stuffing their lives with men. I'd hate to be a passion in the brain of that Eurona. I'd so hate it, that I'd rather be a doorkeeper in the house of the Lord, and the Labour Exchange will tell you I'm no fit man to be a doorkeeper. A passion in the brain of Eurona will be stumbling about in a lot of darkness, fierce, sincere stumbling that will drop her like a ton of aching bricks over every pebble her foot will strike against. Whatever dream she gets she has to have in a bed she shares with four other little kids, each ready to rip her dream to tatters with a squeal of protest at any movement of hair or finger. And if ever she wanted a man to look at her, first she'd have to throw off all her clothes and present him with what the newspapers call an accomplished fact just to make him forget that the clothes she usually wears are older, dirtier and uglier than that abandoned coal mine down there in the valley. When love comes to Eurona, it will, no doubt, be a sticky mess. Her feelings have so little room to move about in and so little faith in their own power to feel themselves remarkable and worthy of respect, her passion will have the same degree of balance as a pyramid stuck on its head... I suggest that we now sing on a soft note the well known anthem of the half-damned, not because I feel like singing but to give us the warm feeling that such things will not always be.'

So we sang, to the future and for the safe passage through womanhood of Eurona's still immobilised passions.

*****

And to Eurona, love came. We found that she chose, for this first trial run, a youth named Rollo, a bus conductor and a great figure in the Terraces. We found also that her affection for this youth went off sharply, in the manner of a firework. You might ask how a bus conductor could ever be considered a great figure. Not knowing the Terraces, you could very well ask that question. In a place that has known only a steady development of wealth and well-being, where the natives do not have to spend so much time away from home agitating for a healthier social philosophy they sometimes commit bigamy through absent-mindedness, a bus conductor would not rate for much. He would be overlooked by all wealthy citizens. They would either put him down as a uniformed serf, or, never using buses, would know of him not at all. But in the Terraces, where State-controlled poverty had such longstanding pillars as Morris, ourselves and the bulk of the other voters whose living as miners had vanished long since through a crack in the floor of the Stock Exchange, the peaked cap, the thick serge suit and the various badges of the bus conductor made him an aristocrat – a king, or at least, a noble, subordinate in dignity and power only to the landlord or to the chap who, also in a peaked cap and a very strong suit of clothes, came poking about on behalf of the Water Board when that Board was worried about our taps and pipes.

Many parents, had they been able to find the devil, which was difficult in so naturally crowded and devilish a place as the Terraces, would have sold him all the soul they had and felt well quit of it, had the devil been able to wangle for their sons a job on the buses. But this bus company was so powerful in the crippled valley we thought they probably had the devil himself working as a wheel-greaser on piece rates in their main garage and developing a soul of his own through wage labour and not liking same. The bus conductors had, as we in the Terraces saw, pleasant work and the kind of opulent security that the average human could only glimpse in vision if he was a little drunk or crazy. The idea of being able to roll about all day in those sublime double-deckers was fascinating to the large mass of Terrace dwellers who only got a taste of travel when they ran behind the buses for a mile or two to smell the petrol. And when the buses swept in swift strong pride up and down the valley, many were the doorsteps on which stood housewives and maidens, waving their aprons, ogling desperately or standing stiffly and solemnly to attention to greet the passing of their favourite conductor. One girl made a stir by throwing herself under a bus to bring her passion to the attention of her particular Romeo who punched his tickets, called out his stops and did his duty altogether too diligently ever to have given her a glance, but we heard later that this girl had always been clumsy in her methods and this under-the-bus episode only came as the climax of a lot of steady work in the same field.

So, you see, the bus conductors were idolised, cherished, sought after, and none more so than this Rollo. He was a pretty type, about twenty-three. He had waves in his hair, very deep fixed waves, that looked as if they had been fixed with a solution of syrup and granite. Rollo wore his peaked cap at a sharp angle, whenever he did not have it off to stroke and show off his waves, which was often. Rollo was one of fifteen who were still working in our Terrace which was the Terrace the Slump actually started out from in 1923, as the plaque we put up on the last house of the row will tell, and Rollo was the only one of that gallant fifteen who wore a peaked cap and could afford three suits and upwards of three hundred waves. This success went to Rollo's head. He was made much of by his parents and relatives who regarded Rollo as a kind of Messiah or Golden Boy. They conversed less and less with their poorer neighbours after Rollo got his job on the buses and conversed more and more on the subject of Rollo. These parents and relatives carried their worship of Rollo to a great height and often went down as a body to a point overlooking the main road of the valley and raised many hearty cheers as Rollo's bus went by. Naturally, Rollo being weak on the mental side, all this success and cheering went to his head and more than once we saw contempt blazing from his blue eyes as he passed groups of voters who were feeling the depression very sharply, like a draught in the neck, and who looked as if they were now carrying the depression around with them instead of having it clip them periodically across the skull, as before.

Rollo even got to the stage where he read scraps of Fascist literature and had been heard at one of the bus stops referring to socialism as a canker and averring that only strong-man government could save the country. The strong man whom Rollo had in mind for this job of saving was an Inspector on the buses, a man with no brain at all, a face as flat and hard as the front of a slate quarry and a solid block of authoritarian truculence from his knee caps to the top of his head. Long before we had thought of Rollo in connection with Eurona, my friend Ben had asked us whether it would not be a good idea to take this Rollo to one side one day and talk some sense into him, as he was, by all standards, a menace. Knowing Ben's great strength and his weakness for falling into violent habits in conversation with menaces, especially menaces like Rollo who flashed contempt for the local voters from his blue eyes and proposed supreme powers for such a low grade piece of handcarved blockheadedness as that Inspector, we told Ben that it would be better if he did not take Rollo to one side, better for Ben and better still for Rollo.

So, we were saddened when we heard that our young friend, Eurona, had taken to making round sad eyes at this Rollo. Not only because he had fallen into vile ways of thinking regarding the political situation but also because the favoured position, the pretty face and the waved hair of this Rollo made him more than popular among the maidens. Rollo had only to wink and a maiden would fall and he winked so often it was getting difficult to see a perpendicular maiden in the Terraces any more. And this Rollo, taking much pride in his god-like status, reserved his attentions only for those maidens who were well turned out, and there was great activity among the seamstresses of the Terraces as they produced dresses for their daughters and friends of a pattern and design sufficient in beauty to rivet the eye of Rollo to one place and lead him to think of marriage.

All that Eurona could do was look at this Rollo. Never in a thousand years could she have worked up the courage to throw him a glance or talk to him. Rollo, to Eurona, was a Mount Olympus with a waved top. All the best dressed Salomes of the Terraces thronged around Rollo, and Eurona stood well beyond the outskirts of this crowd. We got her to talk to us about it, not because we agreed with wasting our time discussing fruitless things like love, but because we saw that Eurona gave herself some satisfaction just by talking of her fondness for this Rollo. We made a lot of propaganda against Rollo to see if that would ease her and set her mind in healthier tracks. But we soon found that she was not to be shaken, that she was, in her attitude to Rollo, only a hair's breadth divided from that party of relatives who went down to the point overlooking the main road of the valley to cheer Rollo's bus as it passed. My friend Ben reported to her that Rollo had been heard to say that under strong-man government, subjects like Morris would be operated on to prevent them from breeding litters of paupers. Eurona said Ben must have heard wrongly; anyway, she added, there might be something in what Rollo said. We thought it was a poor look out for Morris if even his own daughter agreed that his one remaining right and interest should be snipped off to save the Unemployment Fund a shilling or two. My friend Arthur pointed out to her that Rollo had become a kind of buck steer as a result of his popularity among the women, making his affections as much of a public service as the buses he punched tickets for and, therefore, not worth competing for. At this, Eurona opened her eyes wide and looked as if she were going to be sick and then said that though men love many times, they give their hearts but once. That was our turn to look sick and we asked her from what source she had gathered that pearl. She mentioned one of those women's magazines that were given to women when they had the vote to stop them using the vote. We said she ought to be beaten about the head for reading and believing such backward stuff as that. Her answer to this was a deep sigh and a remark that men like us did not understand.

When she saw us looking hurt at this, she hurried to say that we were certainly strong on the Industrial Revolution and the rent question and the beginnings of things, none stronger, but weak on love. Very weak on love. She also said, to finish off the argument for that evening, that whenever she thought of Rollo, she never felt cold and that made my friend Walter say that that proved again that most of the love in this world reflected little more than a shortage of food and coal among so many of the voters. We asked Eurona, thinking as she did that this Rollo was the man of the century, a mixture of Pharaoh, Apollo, Jehovah and the Welsh Amalgamated Colliery Company, and going on fire every time she gave him a thought, what she was going to do about it. She would have to do something, we said, because such sloppy notions could not be allowed to remain in the head indefinitely without rusting the inside of the skull. She glanced down at her shoes from which time and wear and Morris' mice had removed the shape, the gloss and the heels. She pursed her lips, cried quietly but intensely and whimpered that she would never tell him of her love. She added that she would carry the secret of it with her to the grave. That sounded strongly to us like something that had just come fresh and steaming from whatever women's magazine serial it was Eurona was brain-slimming with. Then she went home, leaving us on our wall to wonder if it might be Morris himself who was taking in these women's magazines in an effort to find in their correspondence columns a possible cure for life or for the greyness part of it anyway.

'You must admit,' said my friend Walter, 'that next to such things as money and lack of proper grub, this love is a very great power in the land. What boredom and waste and lack of decent occupation there must be in this life for men and women to work up such pain and endure so much bother over a little issue like deciding the destination of their genitals. Look at Romeo and Juliet.'

We looked at Romeo and Juliet, and, from our expressions, we all thought these two subjects regrettable.

'Then there was another pair of beauties I came across in

a book I got out of the Library when somebody told me I was going mad with reading too many pamphlets and that I needed a bit more general culture. This was a Spanish book and very old, judging by the language used by some of the voters in it. It was about a youth named Calisto who scaled a very high wall to get at the woman of his fancy who was called Melibea and who had good looks and some money, though it is doubtful if this Calisto, a great ram, was after anything but the looks. He broke his neck one night climbing this high wall. High walls are all right when you start courting but later on, with love more advanced, high walls and courting do not mix. The girl is upset. She kills herself. I don't remember if she does this by jumping off the wall herself or taking poison but it shows to what some types can be driven when they live in a sloppy world that doesn't bother to teach young people to treat these private issues in a grown-up way. I wonder what it'll drive Eurona to. She seems to be just as much gone on this Rollo as Melibea was on Calisto, though I do not know if Calisto could have been as big a figure in Spain, as a bus conductor in steady employment is in these Terraces, with a peaked cap and two uniforms. This passion will drive her to something because it is the only thing in her life that's moving. Most of the life inside her is at a standstill and most of the life around here is in the same way, so she'll want this love to drive her to something just to give herself the feeling that she is still alive which is very often a feeling that people want to have. How, when or in what direction she will be driven are questions I find every bit as baffling as the mind of her old man, Morris. There aren't any high walls in the Terraces I know of unless she climbs on to Rollo and takes a jump from his highest wave. She can't afford poison and she can't even use the old reservoir since the Council boarded it up to keep the crowds away. This is a very poor place to live in for any subject whose emotions are boiling and calling out for some sort of climax. But Eurona will find some way of moving forward, mark my words.'

Eurona grew sadder as the days went by. Her sadness reached a peak one evening when the youth Rollo marched down our Terraces looking splendid. He wore a new check suit with golfing knickers, very broad and puffy around the legs, which made him beautiful in the eyes of Eurona to a higher degree than ever before. Eurona, in her ecstasy, with her brain being fingered into many strange shapes by the heat of her fancy, pretended to slip and landed at the feet of this fair and knickered baboon with the idea of being warmed by the touch of his tony-red shoes. Rollo leaped back as she rolled towards him, afraid that his golfing knickers would be soiled by contact with so obvious a pauper as Eurona. He strode on disdainful and, no doubt, a bit depressed at living in such a place where young female paupers came shooting out at you in a roll from the pavements. But he cheered up when he realised that he was being stared at by many voters who were lining the pavements and enjoying their first glimpse of such things as golfing knickers. At first the voters thought the dogs might have got at Rollo's trousers and that he was really going around half-clothed. When they saw that the trousers were as the tailor had intended them to be, they were very impressed by this novelty and followed Rollo closely to get the outline of the things firmly fixed in their minds. Henceforth, the needles of the seamstresses were kept busy on the task of fashioning rough versions of these golfing knickers from the pants of fathers unto the second and third half-breeched generations.

Later that same evening, Eurona came to us and said that she was going to leave the Terraces. Remembering the wise words of our friend Walter regarding the driving quality of this love caper, we did not oppose her in this intention. We recognised that Eurona, if she did not take leave of the Terraces, would, with her feelings giving out more heat than the gas works on the subject of this boy Rollo, take leave of her senses, and we had a large enough stock already of voters who had done that without adding a nice little maid like Eurona to the list. True, it pained us to see this steady drift of young workers from the Terraces, a drift that quickened as future prospects of work grew dimmer and we often grew cold as we watched how the Terraces were rapidly becoming a catacomb from which all the reddest, strongest blood had been drained, leaving only those who were too old, too young or too wise to try their future in other places. But what grieved us more than anything was that Eurona was going to leave us, not directly on account of our respected godmother, the Slump, but on account of this unworthy specimen Rollo.

We asked her if she had told her old man about her plans. She said she had not told him and what was more, was not going to tell him because her old man would not know the first thing about how to get her a job and would most likely try to stop her getting one since Morris was very biased in favour of seeing Eurona continue to help with the housework and act as second mother to those smaller Morris kids who were still at home, work on which Morris set great store. We agreed that Morris was no great shakes at planning careers for his kids and we directed Eurona to the Vacancies Counter at the Labour Exchange, (Female Section). We had heard that many jobs in the domestic line were handed over this counter although things always seemed to be either slack or dead on the corresponding counter in the Male side of this building.

We advised Eurona to get hold of a few testimonials from respectable ratepayers to say that her name was, as she said, Morris, and that she could work so hard she had not had even the time to go to gaol, which was another good point in your favour when putting your case to the Vacancies Counter. She took along a note from a preacher which said she could work like a horse and had sung sweetly, off and on, in the Sunday School Choir. We thought the preacher could have toned down this last item a little. He laid so much stress on it it might give the Vacancies Counter the idea that Eurona would refuse point blank to do any cleaning unless she could do it as one of a choir. But there were no difficulties. The Labour Exchange found Eurona a job in less than a fortnight.

She was accepted as a domestic in a large house in the Home Counties, a house kept by some very wealthy voter who was a Justice of the Peace and a master of the fox hounds. The Vacancies Clerk told Eurona she should think herself lucky to have such an appointment as this, and even Mr Morris gave up a lot of his opposition when it was explained to him that Eurona was going to do the cleaning for a man who had something to do with justice and hunted foxes. The point about the foxes made a much bigger impression on Morris than the point about the justice. He might have had the idea that he could eke out his one suit with the skins of dead animals that Eurona would send home by stealth when the hunter was not looking. We could not say that for certain but there is no doubt that the point about the foxes made a deep impression on Morris. The Vacancies Clerk also told Eurona, after giving her a good looking over and coming to the conclusion that she must have sung very sweetly in that Sunday School choir to take the choirmaster's mind off the way she looked, that she would do well to get fitted up with a decent wardrobe before she left, or the particular English gentry with whom she was going to serve would be slinging her out of the Home Counties so fast and far she would land in the Irish Sea.

This wardrobe question baffled Eurona. She knew she looked liked something that had been brought up under a hedge and kept wearing part of the hedge to make it feel at home but she had not realised that a change of outfit would be needed prior to leaving. She thought she could go, be given a uniform to work and just work. She did not know that folks who go in for hiring other folks have a great sense of human dignity and in nothing is this sense so keen as in their insistence that the folks who are hired to do their dirty work shall be neat and spruce in their appearance at all times, especially when they are turning up to do this dirty work because these wealthy folk are kept so busy organising a cleaner world that they have no time for anything but first impressions.

Mr Morris was no less baffled than his daughter. How the hell, he asked us, going so grey with extra perplexity he looked like a silver thread among the black, how the hell was he going to get a new rigout for Eurona? Rent was going up. So was bread and coal and everything else of which the price was not already jammed tight against the roof. The kids were getting hungrier, were thinking out new ways of being hungry that had not been dreamed of before. He was even getting pictures of food he had picked up from a confectioner's rubbish bin hung up in the kitchen just to fool the kids when they got to the point of raising an agitation about the food shortage. The only new clothes they had seen in his house during the past five years were a shawl and an old Army blanket, so old when he got it that moths were now serving periods of conscription in it in two-year shifts. So how was Eurona expecting to have any fresh changes in the face of all these facts? In any case, he told us desperately, he thought Eurona looked very comfortable the way she was.

'Your idea of comfort, brother Morris,' said my friend Walter, 'is original, to say the least. The girl's been walking about in the most ungodly tatters ever since we can remember. And the way she's dressed now puts me in mind of that age of confusion and dread which is forecast in the Book of Apocrypha, a book I have heard of but have not read. You leave it to me, Morris. I'll get clothes for Eurona.'

Morris looked pleased at this as if he expected my friend Walter to go straightaway into his house and come out bearing a large bundle of women's clothes. But we knew Walter to be a chaste type of man who kept no such things as women's clothes or even women on his premises. So we were not surprised when our friend Walter made no move.

'How will you get them?' asked Morris.

'I'll tell you how to get them. You go to the Assistance Board, explain the case and they'll give you a grant to buy clothes for Eurona to go away in.'

Morris did not like this proposal at all. The Assistance Board was the body that decided how much weekly relief we should get and to which needy voters went for special redress when in particular need. Morris stood in great awe of this body, as most others did, because the Board was as often as not made up of shrewd, efficient men who got their idea of what need was from books and never saw eye to eye with us at all on any aspect of this problem of need. We believed, for an instance, that we did not need an Assistance Board. They did and they got their point, which shows how little use there is in not seeing eye to eye with people if it is only their eye that is taken into account.

'I won't go to the Board,' said Morris, very firmly, for Morris.

'Why not? You're her father. Why not?'

'Because, as I stand now, I get on very well with the Board. I am always civil with the bloke who comes around once monthly to see about my circumstances and I get on very well with them. But if I go to them and say that I want them to fix my daughter up fancy to go away, they will think I am trying to impose on their good nature and they won't like me for it. If they give me a grant at all, they'll take it back in instalments from my dole and then I'll be poor for the rest of my life. I'm not going short for the rest of my days just to let Eurona go away and clean the boots of any foxhunter.'

We would have liked to laugh at the strangeness of Morris' economic notions but we did not laugh because we have found that men's notions of economics get quainter the more they are laughed at, and if there is one thing that lands men as a body in the swamp faster and deeper than anything else, it is a quaint notion of economics. So we sat there solemnly and gazed at Morris as he stood protesting that he had no intention of giving up any part of his wealth for Eurona.

'All right. I'll go to the Assistance Board for you,' said Walter. 'So if their feelings are in any way hurt by the grasping qualities of the unemployed and underprivileged, it's against me they will be feeling hurt and their ancient love for you, Morris, will remain the same.'

Now my friend Walter was a man familiar at all points with the activities of this Assistance Board. To many of the voters in the Terraces, voters with minds like Morris, afraid of everything and with some reason because everything at some time or another seemed to have kicked them hard in the rear, this Assistance Board was a kind of Ark of the Covenant without any curtains on it, a mystery to be approached only with trembling reverence and a series of obeisances and hosannahs that you learned from the handbook they gave you when you first started learning to be a social problem. There was so much trembling done by the voters in front of the offices of this Board, you would think sometimes, on busy mornings, that it was the palsy ward of a large infirmary. Therefore, this Board had an easy time dealing with the bulk of the applicants who came to it because they would be shivering too much to talk clearly and so overpowered by the loud voices, tricky accents, clean shirts and fancy ties of the men who interviewed them and assessed their needs they would not have had much to talk about even if they were not shivering.

But my friend Walter did not belong to this order of men. He kept what little shivering he did for such larger mysteries as pain and war and death and progress. His kind of wisdom was a high one because it was set atop the felt sufferings of many people who formed a brotherhood of which he was a part and upon that wisdom he set himself as upon a mountain. The Assistance Board looked very low therefore to my friend Walter and he treated it without any great respect. Many of the voters who got tongue-tied when they appeared before the Board requested my friend Walter to appear for them and he would put their cases neatly, crisply, strongly, so that these voters would very often be surprised a little later on when the Board would make them a grant for such useful commodities as blankets and beef extracts, good for lessening the cold and smoothing one's passage through the dark. There was a certain amount of blackmail mixed up in this success of my friend Walter and he used this blackmail without blinking an eyelid because very often the Board would fail to see a scrap of need in cases where my friend Walter could see nothing else. The Board knew that if they spurned the oratory and pleas for compassion of Walter and went withholding blankets and beef extracts from people whom Walter proved to be much worse off than any of the sheep or kine from which these blankets and extracts came, he would go thereupon through all the highways and byways of the Terraces with a box to talk on and with a few very hard, hot sentences, would work up much feeling against the Board among the voters, such feeling that there would be a body of voters outside the office of the Board later that day showing the Board how much their feelings had been hurt.

'But you leave my name out of it, Walter,' said Morris when he was persuaded that something might be gained from a visit to the Board. 'I stand on very good terms with the Board, as I said, and I would not like those terms to be disturbed by any foolishness of yours.'

When Morris left us, Walter said it might be interesting to have two strings to our bow and to make an application to that New Age group which sometimes brightened up the appearance of the poor with packages of old clothes. We had been told that this group occasionally made small money grants in the way of pocket money to young people under twenty who were leaving home for the first time to try for work in other parts.

So Walter appeared before a meeting of the New Age Group the next day to plead Eurona's case. There was a lot of palaver and my friend Walter grew very heated when some old maiden who wore so many furs she looked as if she had butchered a menagerie said in a very ho-ho-he-he kind of tone that Walter seemed to have the idea that the group had the means to rig up Eurona to look like a beauty chorus. This remark had been thrown at Walter because he had demanded flatly as soon as he went in that the group

32

would find itself more than halfway to the New Age if they gave Eurona enough to be refitted from stem to stern. The fur woman had no doubt seen something dirty and vulgar in that stem to stern expression. Walter decided to stand no nonsense from this fur woman and said that Eurona had worn so few clothes for so long now she had fooled even a South Sea missionary who had called around the Terraces into addressing her in the talk of Tahiti, which is very short-frocked talk; that if the ho-ho-ing woman could only see Eurona, she would scale off a foot layer of her own furs and present it to Eurona as a foundation garment; also, that since it was necessary that the children of the Terraces should have to leave the Terraces to earn a living, it was only right and fair that they should leave for new lands dressed in such a way as to impress upon the foreigners that it was a human life they wanted to earn a living for.

The group said they would like to see Eurona. We had her in waiting downstairs. We took her up. The fur woman sniffed at the sight of her but those of the group who had outgrown the sniffing stage awarded her a pocket money grant of seven and six almost without a second look. Walter asked the group whether they could not also contribute a few pockets to put all this grant in. The fur woman protested. She said it was this careless dispensing of charity, this rule of the heart and not the head that had driven the country off gold, and she twitched her furs closer about her as she said that as if the restored gold standard was hidden somewhere among them. She also said that rather than permit any further extravagance which might turn the little girl's head and turn her into a strumpet, a Messalina (the wife of the Italian dictator, don't you know, ho-ho), she would be prepared to see every primrose of the Primrose League dyed crimson with her blood. My friend Walter just said why not in a pleased way and left the office, knowing that he would not get a penny more out of these New Age people unless he got Eurona to make her next appearance before them riding naked on a horse, like Godiva, which would be hard, since Eurona, though poor, honest and clean about her person, was, for all these good qualities, no horsewoman.

Then Walter made his way to the Assistance Board. The officer who interviewed him was tired after a morning full of complicated assessments and was in no mood for any lengthy banter with Walter on the social question. So he listened to all that Walter had to say and looked up all the papers he had regarding Morris, which took some time because there were many papers regarding Morris in one part of the building and another, Morris, as I have mentioned, being a very famous figure in this institution of relief. The officer said he thought a grant of two pounds for clothing might very well be made. Not enough, said Walter, and argued that Eurona had been going about practically naked for so long now the Board should allow her three of each kind of garment, as a kind of back pay, to make up for lost time. The officer looked a lot less tired when he heard these arguments and told Walter that he was greatly deluded if he thought the Board had any notion of branching out as a sort of wardrobe department for the dispossessed and that he would cancel even the two pounds grant if Walter did not stop being a pest and a drag on the efficiency of the Government. So my friend Walter said so be it and stopped being a pest and went his way, leaving the Government to be efficient.

The following evening, we staged a little concert in the wooden hut we had built for ourselves at the top of the Terraces. We built this hut from wood we had salvaged from a fire-gutted cinema where we had seen so many rotten shows we thought the timber was owing to us. We found this hut useful, small as it was. It belonged to us and that alone made it remarkable. So little belonged to us. It was a place where we could hold meetings and concerts for which we would not have been able to get a larger hall where a fee was needed. The cinema contractor had once tried to reclaim the timber of the hut. We refused. He became very angry, as all contractors do at the sight of any timber they consider to be theirs. One night he made an effort to get it back in the middle of a concert we were holding and managed to bring one of the ceiling beams down on the head of a very nice baritone called Waldo Parry, who was halfway through a difficult song about Prince Llewelyn fighting in the Snowdon district. Waldo was upset at the idea of any man pulling a beam down on his head and, made very martial already in his outlook by the song about Prince Llewelyn which was all about Welsh guerrilla fighters, he went out of the little hut and threw the cinema contractor over it before coming back to finish off his song.

We decided to arrange this latest concert in the hope of making a few shillings for Eurona who would be needing various odds and ends necessary to maidens which she would not be able to afford to buy out of the grants that had been made her by the Board and the New Age Group. For this concert we gathered all the talent in the Terraces that could be gathered at such short notice. We had my friend Ben playing a large piano accordion which he had borrowed from some friend who intended playing this instrument in the street when he could find a street big enough to hold the volume. That accordion had much volume. Every time Ben squeezed the thing hard and got all the sound he could from it, the ushers had to stand on tip toe, or, if they were short, stand on chairs and hang on to the roof, the roof being weak with regard to nails and plugs and never meant to hold such a blast as came from this accordion.

Then we had little Wilfred, a small man, who looked like a gnome and who sang songs from Italian operas and he would have sung them very well if he could have remembered all the words and music. He could not remember. That was the failing that had kept little Wilfred hanging about the Terraces. There was nothing wrong with his voice. It was a strong, clear voice with a streak of passion a yard thick, just a little less thick than Wilfred was tall, and his singing never failed to please all the people that turned up to the concerts we held in the small hut. But Wilfred could never remember for more than six bars what he was supposed to be singing about and that had kept him off the stage viewed as a job; on top of that he looked too much like a gnome. He made up for this by turning on the full strength of his voice every time he felt himself fumbling over the words and music. The more he fumbled the louder he sang; so the few seconds before Wilfred finally realised that he was beaten and sank to rest were always very noisy seconds during which you could imagine you had a whole choir opening out just inside your ear. Wilfred on a top note and Ben going full blast on his accordion, put on together, would have had the whole audience floating over the mountain and bawling down to the Assistance Board for an emergency grant to buy parachutes.

Then my friend Walter, in a sweet, soft voice sang some Irish songs such as 'Believe me, if all those endearing charms' with harmonies from Ben and myself when he came to the refrain and we made twenty-five people in the two front rows burst out crying because they were near enough to get the full flavour of these harmonies which, containing as they did the marrow of most of the emotions we had, were rich and pleasing. The people in the audience were very surprised to hear my friend Walter soothing them with these gentle and harmless lyrics of Tralee and Mourne for they knew him mainly as a man who went around top-heavy with pamphlets and practically bowed double by the heavy thought he gave to the social question and bulging with facts and saying keen things about the economic position and Governments. But we have usually found in the Terraces that the man who has the sense to put his clothes out of shape by carrying pamphlets around, has the sense to do quite a number of other things well besides.

Then I got up and recited some Chartist hymns with plenty of fire and gestures and pauses. These poems did not make much sense to a group of neighbours sitting on one of the back benches. These people had bright eyes and were Apostolic Christians and they were sitting on the back benches because they had been driven in from the streets by the cold and were not too sure what was going on. They were looking uncomfortable as I did my recitations because, no doubt, they thought from the fierce tone of these Chartist items and the way I threw my arms about and set my jaw during the pauses that they had stumbled into a political meeting. These Apostolic elements, of course, are forbidden to attend political meetings. They are above politics and above most other things, too. So, for their benefit, I finished off my recitations with a rendering of 'The Private of the Buffs', with a full set of actions that got the Apostolics thoroughly thawed out and the two front rows, occupied in the main by backward voters who looked as if they had come along prepared to enjoy the thing to the full even if it had turned out to be an indoor burial, on their feet and stamping applause.

At the end of my recitation, my friend Walter rose and explained to the audience that this Buff I had been carrying on about, though no doubt deserving the normal amount of sympathy which is coming to those who have their heads chopped off and their bodies thrown on to a dung heap, had, all the same, been a mercenary in the pay of foreign overlords in China, doing hard things in an unthinking spirit to the Chinese people and deserving all he got, being rough and drunk, so drunk he even dreamed of hopfields, as well as being a mercenary. Somebody in the middle of the hut said 'Long live the Chinese brethren' and my friend Walter looked pleased when he heard that but he bent over to where I was sitting and whispered in my ear that I deserved to come to an even stickier end than the Buff Private if I got up and recited any more ballads in favour of imperialism.

When the biggest part of all this singing and reciting had been done, my friend Arthur, who had a very kindly way with him when he was not worried by his ulcer, stood up as chairman and explained that this concert had been arranged at short notice to raise a few shillings for little Eurona who had already got a clothing grant from the Assistance People by reason of wishing to leave the Terraces and work for a foxhunter. Arthur got sentimental in his remarks, which was ever a sound tactic in such mixed gatherings as concerts where you never know what elements you might have stuck away on the back benches, driven in by the weather. He told how the Terraces had suckled Eurona and we all thought to ourselves, without any disrespect, that she looked like it. He said Eurona was a child of the Terraces and now, hungry for a fuller, finer, richer, more colourful life, (my friend Arthur seemed to have taken some kind of postal lessons in adjectives), she was going to leave all those who loved her so well and was going to take her place as an obscure, nameless, unsung worker in the great city of London or somewhere about there.

We all looked very sad when we pondered over this oratory and Eurona who sat in the very front row, cried into some part of her coat that she seemed able to pull clean away from the main body of it and then fix back again. Probably, she had grown to like us in some fashion and we thought she might have some reason for that, because, although we were and looked pretty useless from

39

the viewpoint of wealthy citizens, we still had a lot of such good points as patience, good temper and the power to talk the world halfway off its axle... Arthur added that already the Terraces had sent a stream of their young people out into the world and now Eurona was going to join the stream. That stream was our blood for it meant that the community we had built up in the Terraces, and a warm, cheerful, striving community it had been in the days that were gone, would now pass away and leave no trace, for those boys and girls, since we, the older ones, had lost most of our usefulness, were the only link we had with the future. So, we would all give as generously as we could to Eurona, not only to send her away from the Terraces with a smiling memory of people who were nearly forgetting the way to smile, but to make our kindness to her a message to all the lads and girls whom we had bred but who would never be seen among us any more.

When the collection caps went around there was a lot of eager jumping up and searching into pockets by the audience and there was as much borrowing one from the other as ever you would see in a Stock Exchange or a Bank. We collected twelve and six. When we had counted it, my friend Ben blew out a great blast on his accordion and said it was a miracle but he hurried to tell us that when he said anything was a miracle he was not surrendering an inch of his ground on the religious question, which was fiercely anti-miracle. The most likely reason for the collection being so big was that the night was Saturday and the week that was composed of seven days had not yet reached its point of deepest gloom.

The audience was thanked for this effort. The gathering of twelve and six, said my friend Arthur, from a small meeting of people so poorly situated with regard to collections as we were, would remain as a milestone on the hard road to freedom we were treading. One last item was called for. We selected little Wilfred, the tenor, whose memory was so bad and who looked like a gnome. We selected him because he was hanging about the piano and eager, by his look, to keep singing, with intervals for forgetting, till the dawn. We took little Wilfred to one side and got him to tell us if there was one song, any song that he was sure he could sing without a break from beginning to end. Oh yes, said Wilfred, he knew the 'Holy City', backwards, forwards, upwards, downwards. He said that very emphatically, as if to say we should have been able to tell by the very look of him that he had this mastery over the 'Holy City'. So we turned him loose on 'The Holy City' with a feeling of great confidence, although Walter said that a song like 'The Holy City' coming right on top of a bit of cow's heel like the 'Private of the Buffs' would send the audience home in such a primely reactionary state of mind there would probably be a pogrom in the Terraces on the following day and processions of voters marching through the streets demanding less dole, higher taxes and the Stuart monarchs.

Little Wilfred got through the first verse of 'The Holy City' very well but the second verse he sang was the first verse of a different song which had a name something like 'Volunteers Bold Are We'. Wilfred did no fumbling at all to mark this change. He took it in his stride and switched over

41

to this other song as calmly as you will. The pianist, tired by now of Wilfred's unsteady method of building a programme, refused to have any truck with this medley and kept to the 'Holy City'. Between little Wilfred going all out with the Volunteers and the pianist playing 'The Holy City' there was a combination of sounds that seemed queer to all except to little Wilfred who enjoyed himself throughout.

On the following Monday, five of us accompanied Eurona to a large store in the main street of the valley where Eurona was going to buy her clothes. We went with her as a kind of bodyguard to see that she would not be swindled and as a sort of judging committee to pass verdict on such details as cut and colour; also, we wanted to pass on an afternoon which would normally have been spent sitting on a wall. In any case, we were interested, the lot of us, in what happened to Eurona who was, in our eyes, one of the leading blossoms of the depression, an orphan of the world crisis, one of us. Morris came with us too. He was very excited as he walked among us because he thought the large store might toss him something in the way of a spoiled garment or a sun helmet to go with the tan he might have if he had any sun to stand in, as a rebate on the many purchases that Eurona was going to make. His greyness was burning to a gleaming white with all this excitement and my friend Ben told him at one point that he looked so much like an electric light with all this gleaming his hand kept looking for the switch.

As we marched into the store with Eurona at our heels and Morris running in circles like a retriever, the manager of the store saw us and started to whistle 'Happy Days', thinking that such a large procession must be the herald of a boom. When we told him we were there, not to lead in a boom but only to spend a voucher from the Assistance Board, he handed us and his smile over to an assistant. Marshalled in single file, we began to make our way around the counters with an eye to bargains. Eurona was all for bright colours and laughed in a high voice that went right around the store without buying anything every time she saw anything bright enough to make you blink. Morris scolded Eurona for this laughing and jumped in a startled way every time she came out with a fresh peal, and he told us it was no doubt the sight of all these new articles lying on the counters that was affecting Eurona like a sunstroke and causing her to giggle in this piercing way.

We took a solemn view of this weakness in Eurona for showing delight at the sight of loud colours. We told her she owed it to the Assistance Board, from which two pounds worth of her blessings had flown, to us, to the Industrial Revolution, to the Terraces, to the mood of the times and to her old man who looked so much like the leg of an old bier, to choose for her clothes only those shades that could be called quiet and dignified and resolute. She bit her lip and let us choose. When she saw that our mania for quietness and dignity was making us pick up everything in the store that was black, except the figures in the cash registers, and that when we had done with clothing her she would very likely look like somebody who has just buried every other voter within a radius of ten miles, she leaned against a pillar and cried. She did not cry quietly but splashed her tears over this pillar as if she were cleaning it.

Morris, who had fancied a suit on one of the stalls, asked us what could be done with a girl as unreasonable as that and suggested that we should pass the voucher over to him to get the suit he had fancied. We had a look at this suit. We had to look at it in stages because it was very blinding. It was a purple colour with thick red stripes that made the purple look as if it had a complaint. This suit, worn in a sombre division like the Terraces, would have brought great eyesight trouble to all those voters who were not already taken over by such eyesight troubles as came with age and astigmatism. We thought it interesting that so grey a voter as Morris should have chosen for his fancy a suit so lively it would have made him look as if he had been dead about three hundred years and wanted to make a mark as the best dressed ghost. We told him sharply to put away this greedy idea of spending Eurona's voucher on himself and added that with his notions and a new suit such as the one described, he would be in the Cabinet in no time at all so the least we could do was keep him away from the suit.

We gave in to Eurona, told her to pick anything she wanted and to hell with quietness and all else. She came away from the pillar in a rush and bought as many as she could buy of the cheapest, brightest garments in the shop. When she held them proudly in her arms in a bundle before they were wrapped up, the mixture of colours in the stuffs jangled like Hungarian Gypsy music played on pots. She also bought a very high-heeled pair of cardboard shoes that we thought would keep the water out just because the heels were so high they kept the biggest part of the cardboard a long way from the ground where most of the water would be. These shoes were shiny, which shows what interesting things man can do with cardboard when he tries, and this shine and smoothness were a great thrill for Eurona who kept rubbing the toes of these shoes over the lower part of her face and humming softly as if the shoes were a kid she wanted to make sleep.

Another item we thought very strange among the things she bought was a thick tube of some stuff called Fixo. This Fixo claimed the power to keep hair so stiff and glossy you would think it was dead if you did not know differently, so stiff indeed if you lifted the hair of one using Fixo you would be lifting the user as well, which seemed to show as high a degree of stiffness as ever you would get from a tube. My friend Ben said he admitted Eurona's hair needed a lot of improving in the way of gloss but he thought we were making a mistake getting this stuff Fixo because the last time he had heard of it was in connection with fixing the tops back on tables, the seats back on chairs and even, but my friend Ben was good enough to admit that he would not swear to this, the roofs back on houses. Walter said we might get rid of all these doubts regarding the functions and powers of this Fixo by trying it out on Morris as a punishment for that greedy thought he had had about spending the voucher on that suit and if he woke up the next day with his head stuck to the ground or standing, legs upward, on the roof, keeping the tiles down for the landlord, we would know Ben was right and would keep Eurona away from this product. But Eurona said she had a friend who had done wonders with this Fixo, making her hair such a mass of gloss she could read by the gleam of it if she kept her head close enough to the paper, and she would use it herself with pleasure.

We said all right and to give Eurona a few more pushes in the direction of that beauty they seem to think so much of in the Home Counties, we bought her from our own pockets a few threepenny tins of face powder and skin cream from which great beauty is said to arise to the faces of those maidens who can afford as many of these threepenny tins as they like. Morris was very taken up with the look of the face cream which was a pinkish, pretty colour and he kept licking his lips at the sight of it. He said he liked the look of it so much he was willing to bet he could eat it on toast. We told him we did not doubt that and promised him that the next time he felt fed up and had a fire big enough for toasting, we would let him have a sixpenny tin of this vanishing cream and he could take his own time over vanishing.

We got Eurona's splendour wrapped up, got the sales receipted for the benefit of the Assistance Board which does not trust the verbal oaths of any voter with too small an income to live for truth alone. Then our procession made its way back to the topmost Terrace where we lived, feeling, all of us, like Santa Claus, but older, thinner and shorter in the wind. Eurona was due to leave in two days time and we told her that we would see her before she went and we would do our final duty by escorting her to the station. From that point forward, she would be simply an invisible speck of that world we worried so much about.

We saw her the next day. It was middle evening when we saw her. It was that part of day when most of the voters in the Terraces retire into their homes, to brood in their many ways on what a hell of a day it has been and God forbid that tomorrow will be the same, a time of day when the streets are mostly empty, save for little groups of boys and girls who stand around lamp posts and shop windows singing at each other and girding their loins and so on for a game with passion. Eurona crept along shyly from the house to the yard where she knew she would find us. She was clad in every stitch of her new finery and she had her hair plastered with what must have been a record thickness of Fixo, leaving out the girl Eurona had said did most of her reading by the gleam of it. In addition, she had a nice coating of face cream and powder, almost speaking with its whiteness, standing out as vividly as song against silence, hunger against wealth, life against death, on the raven gleam of the Fixo.

There was so much yellow in her costume we thought a flock of canaries must have got loose in the Terraces and, indeed, there was the song of canaries in the voice of Eurona as she talked to us, for she was very happy. She asked us if we liked the way she looked. We examined her in detail and were breathless at such a change for, with a few ounces of extra flesh, Eurona would have been the spitting image of that Theda Bara whose eyes and lips and hips had warmed us through many a winter evening in that cinema which had been destroyed by a fire, started no doubt by some over-heated patron in the front rows who had taken Theda too much to heart. Earnestly, we told Eurona that, dolled up in this yellow and glossy fashion, she was a credit to her class as a whole and to the Terraces part of it in particular, that

47

we had never seen so little yellow used to spice so vast a feast of beauty, that we had seen nothing so handsome or so moving since that Pageant of History we had staged in the valley two winters before in which we carried banners bearing the portraits of all the world's boldest proletarians from Wat the Tyler to Mao-Tse-Tung.

And we meant with our hearts all we said to Eurona for even to men who have lived much of their lives in simple endurance and expectation of sadness and strife, the sight of beauty, however frail, tawdry and soon to perish it might be, is very pleasant if they themselves have had a hand in the making of it. The happiness of Eurona was something we had helped create, we who have desired to create so much and have created so little. The sight of it, the nearness of it to the very centre of our cold, spoiled lives warmed us, gave us a brilliant moment's glimpse, that nearly made us weep, of the larger happiness that men like us would like to bring to all the world we live in. The glimpse was a fragment of the vision we have seen so clearly and so constantly in all the hopes that have arisen like sentinels over our present state, that we have come to know in all its smallest and most lovely details, in the prophetic urges that often come to minds too much alone and scorned, as well as we would come to know some brother greater than ourselves, yet to be born, bringer of full reckoning, joyful rebirth. All this we expressed to Eurona with a few curt sentences.

'Oh Christ, Eurona, you look grand.'

'The depression's over.'

'We've turned that corner the papers talk about.'

'O Beulah land.'

Having heard how satisfied we were, Eurona went home, herself satisfied in a way that made all her limbs to tremble and her body to sway.

We saw her again the next night. She was still wearing her new clothes and we thought she must have taken such a fancy to these garments she was sleeping in them. But we saw that her face looked different. She looked as if someone had been pumping her eyes up and as no one in the Terraces had yet reached the stage where they wanted to pass the time on by blowing other people's eyes up, we guessed she had been crying. Since she was going away on the following day, we did not consider this unnatural. Even a voter like Morris would be hard to leave if you were his kid. Also, the only previous occasion on which Eurona had been away from the Terraces was with a Sunday School trip to the sea side, so she had very little experience of going away from the Terraces.

'No need to cry, Eurona,' said my friend Walter. 'No need to cry because you are going away tomorrow. The Terraces will always be here to welcome you back if you get sick of it where you are going. In any case, you'll probably like it away from here because these Terraces are no place for young people any more. They are washed out and they are old and they have no future.'

'I'm not going away tomorrow,' said Eurona and her mouth opened as wide as her eyes. She was smiling. We gave ourselves two or three minutes to take in this bit of news. We had gone to some trouble to prepare Eurona for her going away but we never thought of throwing such facts in her face. As far as we are concerned, men and women are free to do as they please but we have noticed many other people with a great pull in the community who do not share this view and we have to be cautious, therefore, not to go steering any of our friends into gaol by urging them to follow their fancy under all circumstances especially when some of these circumstances might turn out to be a batch of those experts mentioned above who have a great pull and have views opposite to ours and a taste for measuring their own value and importance in terms of the numbers of those they manage to get put away for such things as free speech and fleshly capers. So we felt bound to ask Eurona what had led her to this surprising decision to stay in the Terraces when there was a foxhunter in the Home Counties who was probably suffering from dirt and neglect for the lack of her.

'And why aren't you going away tomorrow, Eurona?' asked my friend Arthur.

'Because last night,' said Eurona, smiling so much now she was no more than eyes and mouth beneath a roof of Fixo. 'Rollo saw me. Rollo talked to me. Rollo told me I was the nicest girl he had ever seen in the Terraces. Rollo said he loved me. Rollo left Millicent Jefferies to take me for a walk.'

'Who the hell is Millicent Jefferies?' asked my friend Ben, but we invited Ben with our eyes to be silent because we felt that questions about such subsidiary issues as this girl Jefferies were neither here nor there and would help us in no way at all.

'And you aren't going away?' asked Walter.

'I only wanted to go away because Rollo wouldn't talk to me. Now that Rollo has talked to me and kissed me, why should I want to go away?'

We gave one another long looks as if to say that if the twists and turns of life were to be dictated by such lads as Rollo, then life was going to become very tricky for the many voters who are simple-minded and that life might be sold off there and then to anyone wanting to do a deal in years and hopes, sold off cheap. But we said nothing of this straightaway to Eurona. There was a lot of logic in what she said and we were worshippers of logic.

'This Rollo,' said my friend Arthur, more to himself than to Eurona, 'seems to be a man who is quick to observe things. One day he passes you by as if you were one of the road's larger pebbles, refuses, if I remember your story rightly, to even touch you with his tony-red shoe. The next day, when you've tidied yourself up a bit, he swarms to you as flies to treacle. He has decided now, no doubt, to give you both his tony-red shoes to rub yourself against. It's a sudden and surprising change. Between Rollo and my stomach, I feel very giddy.'

'It was the Fixo,' said my friend Ben. 'There must be some charm connected with that Fixo. Look at the way her hair is gleaming now. You've got to admit it is pretty beyond.'

We all had a look and said we admired the shiny blackness of Eurona's hair.

'And I owe it all to you,' said Eurona and she clapped her hands together hard, as kids do to show their delight.

'Owe all what?'

'Being happy. If it hadn't been for you, for all the lovely clothes you got me from that shop, perhaps Rollo would never have noticed me.'

'There is nothing more certain than that,' said Walter. 'These clothes gave you life, Eurona, and life is a lot to buy with two pounds odd. It says a hell of a lot when just that amount of money can stand between somebody being dead and being alive. But the point is, Eurona, that you would not have had these clothes and you would still be dead if we hadn't gone along to the Assistance Board and explained that you were going away to work.'

'Oh, you just tell them I changed my mind.' Eurona's voice had a speed, a balance, a confidence that she had never had in her voice before. We were impressed to hear any element showing such ignorance of the character of the Board as to wish to transmit to it such a carefree message as Eurona had just transmitted. It promised well for the future and we were glad but it ached a bit in the present and that gave us some sorrow.

'Eurona, the Assistance Board does not like people who change their minds. They are not interested in minds at all but only in needs. They're not interested in you looking pretty for Rollo or in the fact that you spent months crying your eyes out because you were not looking pretty for Rollo. All they want you to do is look pretty for that foxhunter in the Home Counties whose house you are going to keep clean for him and the foxes. We've got no objection to you staying here for life and being loved by Rollo. We can't say we're all for Rollo. Personally, we consider Rollo to have a brain so weak you could not even make broth from it. We don't like the way his eyes flash from maiden to maiden. We don't like the way his hair waves up and down. Neither can we say that we are all for love as such. We consider love to be very over-rated, a great waster of time and a hindrance to deeper understanding among the voters. But we're all for your being happy. That's why you've got to listen now to what we have to say. If you suddenly lost those clothes and you had to turn up in front of Rollo dressed in those ancient rags you wore before, you would not be so popular with Rollo, would you, he wouldn't be so quick to say he loved you and leave that Millicent in the lurch in order to do so, would he?'

Eurona took her time over answering that. At first, we thought she would come out with some fresh pellet of women's magazine whitelead, like love being blind and about Rollo not caring any more what she looked like now that he had seen the real her. Had such a pellet come, we would have changed both sex and faith and become nuns. But we had imparted too much honest materialism to Eurona for her to fall into such deep error. Her answer was to wrap her new clothes more tightly around her and to say fiercely: 'I'd like to see anybody trying to take my clothes away from me'.

'All right, Eurona. You do what you like. You'll find quite a body of persons in this world who will make it their duty to stop you doing what you like, so we will not join up with that crew. We only oppose people we've got nothing in common with. You and we have a whole worldful of troubles in common. But if you don't go away tomorrow to that job the Vacancies Counter found for you, there will be some new kind of trouble we haven't tasted yet. People who hand out money and clothes for the Government are very narrow-minded about the use made of these articles. They don't take love into account as far as I can see. They might think highly of love, might even cry over the subject as you and some others do, but they can't be bothered with it when they are doing the handing out for the Government. If Romeo had gone to the Assistance Board for a special poison grant when he found that all was vain and then the Board discovered after making the grant that Romeo had decided not to even taste this poison, they would have had angry words with him, maybe forced the stuff down his throat and stopped any plays being written about him. So if you are not going away tomorrow, either you'd better say you're ill and send the clothes back to the shop or you can keep the clothes and give back to the Board and the New Age Group all the money they gave you. God, I'd like to see that fur woman's face if I went and told her you had decided to turn down the foxhunter in the cause of liberty and passion. I bet she'd show more teeth and swish a longer tail than all the animals she skinned to get those furs.'

'We haven't got any money to pay anybody back,' said Eurona. 'You know my father. He's never got much money. You know that.'

'What are you going to do?'

'I'll stay home with Rollo and I'll keep my clothes,' said Eurona with all the defiance in the world, and ran off.

We settled ourselves down on the brick wall and considered this question in silence, each of us, no doubt, thinking it much more interesting than that tale of the two

Spaniards, Calisto and Melibea, which had been told us by our friend Walter.

'It's a hell of a world,' said my friend Ben but we all knew that and it was not such a fact as would help Eurona's problem, that problem being that it was just such a hell of a world. All the same, we thanked Ben for his statement as being, without question, sincere and from the heart.

'What a business it is,' said Walter. 'The Assistance Board steps in like a fairy godmother and rigs Eurona out in a selection of stripes that make her look like a barber's pole. This Rollo, seeing these stripes and being, I suppose, partial to barbers, exchanges a few words with her regarding love and that opens out all the gates of heaven to Eurona. Some people choose quaint heavens but that is their business. Nothing of all this would have happened if Eurona had not decided to slope off out of the Terraces and seek a new life elsewhere. The Board will kick up hell when they find that Eurona is making a wrong use of the clothes. They'll kick up hell with us, too, because we practically made ourselves responsible for the girl. When that officer I saw about the grant finds that the only use Eurona wants to make of all her new garments is to play the goat with Rollo, he'll most likely have me put away in the Tower on a charge of trying to introduce a better tailored brand of lust into the Terraces in place of the work that used to be here. We don't mind that. If we haven't got love as a thing to keep us warm, it's just as well to have people kicking up hell at you because there's a lot of warmth in that too. Eurona'll have to try to keep it dark for a spell that she's staying on here. But they'll find out sooner or later unless she can stay off the streets by tunnelling her way to Rollo every time the mood is on her. And then when they do find out she's not gone, they'll make things very unpleasant for her. They've started a new campaign now against people who make false claims and go in for other dishonest practices. I know that because one of the clerks in the offices of the Board told me, on that very subject, that if the poor can't learn to be honest they might as well be dead because no man who goes around making false claims about his means and cheating the Government can hope for the good opinion of his neighbour, and I laughed at that because I couldn't think of one single neighbour whose opinion I gave a damn about. But the trouble, the real trouble is that this little Eurona is going to have a packet any way she turns. Up one alley, she'll run smack into the Board in the middle of their new campaign to make the poor honest and up the other she's going to run into a lot more nights of weeping with regard to this Rollo who'll see Eurona about half a dozen times, stuff her with a lot of nonsense in which a bit of active breeding might well play a part and then he'll hurry on to some other maiden who wears a deeper shade of yellow in her skirt or uses an ounce more Fixo to the square hair than Eurona.'

'Perhaps,' said my friend Ben. 'Perhaps if I were to go and talk to this Rollo, argue with him, even clip him once or twice in such a way as to flatten a few of those waves that must be disturbing his brain, he'd agree to be faithful to Eurona and that would not be so bad. I am all against this Rollo being allowed to go around unscathed doing all this havoc to maidens.'

'No, you can't do that. If you went along and treated Rollo in this way, he'd drop Eurona all the more quickly. You can't tell people who they are to love unless you are in the stud farm business and you, Ben, are in no business at all. In any case, Rollo's parents and relatives are very touchy on the subject of Rollo and if you took even the small part of a wave from Rollo's head, they would have the police at your door in under a minute. No, I do not see myself that there is much we can do for this little Eurona.'

A little later, Morris himself came along. He was moaning as if someone were sticking a knife into him. This moaning made a sad figure of Morris indeed for even when he was not moaning he looked as if he could already see the knife. Eurona had just told him that she had changed her mind about going away and was going to stay. The news, said Morris, had upset him very much, more than he could say. We told him not to say it. Moan it, we said, and we will supply the words. He accused us of having a flippant attitude with regard to grief. We assured him that on this subject of grief we were always very earnest. We urged him to tell us of his worries. The Board, he said, would accuse him, the father, of having planned the whole thing and when they found he could not make a refund of the grant money, they would make an example of him. He asked us in a frightened tone what we thought this example might be.

'Gaol,' said Ben. 'They are getting very strict with voters who take advantage of the Government by such capers as lying and cheating.'

'Oh Christ,' said Morris. 'It's enough to make a man grey.'

'Greyer,' said Ben looking sternly at Morris.

A fortnight passed. We saw Morris every day but not Eurona. He told us he was getting into such a panic he felt he would like to drown himself if he could be put in touch with some deep, clean water. He insisted that this water had to be deep and clean as if he would be letting himself and the Terraces and the Board down very badly if he went jumping into any shallow, dirty stuff. We knew of no such water in the Terraces unless Morris got a bit thinner and managed to work his way up a tap. He had heard that an official of the Board had been around making inquiries as to the whereabouts of Eurona, because the local Labour Exchange had received no confirmation to date of her having arrived at the house of the foxhunter who was no doubt worrying himself bald over having to clean his own foxes. Morris said he had been trying to hide Eurona but she had not been in the house half the time for him to hide her and during those periods he had been hiding himself, and this, he added, was very wearing on a voter like himself who wanted nothing more than to live on frank and friendly terms with the Government. We told him not to worry, and worried a great deal ourselves.

'As if a man like me would want to defraud the Board,' Morris would say every so often and throw his grey little head back in what he thought was a tragic, mocking laugh but which sounded just like the croup to us, as if to say that the very sound of the thought on his lips was enough to drive him out of his wits.

Then, sixteen days after Eurona had first appeared before us in her state-aided finery, we heard that Rollo had now picked up with a young widow who had just come back to the Terraces from London with a fur coat and an English accent and very reactionary views that weighed more, smelled more and had more hair on them than the fur. This young widow, we heard, was buying all-day tickets on the buses just to be within sight and sound of Rollo, which meant that either she was far gone on Rollo or prepared to go to any length to forget her first husband because these buses that Rollo worked on were very rough and jerky and bad on the stomach unless you had your stomach strapped to the seat or to your chest, these two things being very often in the same place when the bus went down a hill at any speed.

One evening, Morris came to us looking most solemn, as if he had just come in from a spell of many years in the wilderness building a church from bits of his own body. We knew that he had come to us with bad tidings of Eurona. We were always reverent in the presence of the life force when it started putting its teeth into other peoples' pants, so we bade Morris in a kind and comradely way to get settled down on one of the bricks of the wall we sat on. He got settled down on half a brick, being small. The expression on Morris' face seemed to say that he had been standing very close to life and looking hard at it, as a rabbit looks at the weasel. A dirtied, unhealthy kind of expression.

He told his tale. The night before, Eurona had come in. She was dressed in her fancy clothes but looked downcast. When the others went to bed, she did not go with them. She waited down. Half an hour later, Morris had been disturbed by the smell of burning cloth. He had hoped first of all that it might be the bedclothes because he was cold and his wife stubborn. He tracked the smell downstairs after a bit of keen tracking on the landing, and he found Eurona sitting absolutely naked in front of the kitchen fire, 'sitting there white and naked with her hair sticking out from the back of her stiff and flat as a bench with that bloody Fixo,' watching the flames rise from her new clothes which she had wrapped into a bundle and dumped on to the fire. Morris had tried to rescue some of these clothes, furious at seeing the property of the Assistance Board being treated in this fashion. But the clothes were well alight and all he obtained from this manoeuvre was a secondary fire started when one of the blazing garments, 'a yellow contraption,' fell on to the canvas hearth mat. He had turned around from this fire-fighting with the idea of belabouring the naked Eurona, 'beating her just as she was, naked like that'. But Eurona had slipped upstairs and there she had remained ever since, lying still on her bed, not even crying, defying all calls, defying even the attempts of Morris to drag her off the bed. We listened attentively and could not imagine Morris doing anything very great in the dragging line.

'And pretty soon,' added Morris with the look and tone of a man whose only remaining job is to count the number of words on the headstone, 'the Board will find out about her not going to that situation with the English gentleman. Then what sort of trouble will I be in? If she stays in that bed, naked, she won't even be in a fit state to go down to the Board and explain to them why she did not go.'

'Bring the Board up to see her,' said my friend Walter.

'The walk will do them good even if they do not draw any other moral from the tale. I'm not thinking of the Board at all at this moment. I'm thinking of Eurona which is what you might be doing too, Morris. Just try looking into her brain and imagine what's going on there. I wish the life force would pick on bigger and tougher bulls-eyes when it takes to playing darts with the voters. Keep an eye on her, Morris, and we'll do all we can to help.'

'Help! The less you try to help me, the safer I'll feel. The Board used to think a lot of me before you chaps started putting ideas about clothes into Eurona's head. Now look at me. No man's my friend and the Board's my enemy.'

'All right, all right, Morris. After the life you've lived, brother, you ought to be hopping about with joy at the very thought of gaol.'

'She must have heard about the widow,' said Ben when Morris had left us.

'Aye. She must have heard of the widow.'

'I don't see, Walter,' said Ben, 'why this Rollo should not be talked to. I feel angry at so many things I could spend a nice half hour flattening Rollo's nose and straightening his hair.'

'That won't do, Ben. This is love, a tricky issue, nowhere as straightforward as politics. If the Assistance tries to make Eurona any more miserable than she is now, we can do something there. We can stand on principle and take strong arguments down to the Board and remind them that if they allow people to go giving up such articles as thrones for the sake of love, surely one of our people can give up a lousy little job for the same good reason. Very widespread, love.

61

Branches all over and, like the proletariat, knows no boundaries, not even Morris' front door which is a boundary for practically everything else I can think of including sense. Oh yes. We can stand between Eurona and the State because that is part of a process essential to our lives. But we cannot stand between Eurona and the bellyaches she might receive from this passion nonsense.'

We turned away, baffled. The life pattern seemed to be getting too blotched to be borne. Eurona's conduct was without that pin-point of clarity we had always tried to press from even the crassest antics of social living. It was no use appealing to Morris to lend a hand. He kept a very tight hold on his limbs. That would have been like turning with hopeful look to some sound the wind might make. Morris had been soaked long since into the fabric of dumb and endured things and was to be perceived now only as a slight stain that had reached the final end of its spreading. Eurona herself was not going to be easy to reason with. We had so few of the weapons that gave men the confidence to take events by the sleeve and mutter commands into their ears that we insisted, before undertaking to help people, that they should be, as a minimum condition, out and about, upright and clothed. Here was Eurona putting herself out of court on every count. She was inside, prostrate and naked, unfit, in all three particulars, for normal intercourse, even in the Terraces.

There seemed little we could do except shrug, realise how limited the arsenal of our means and benevolence had now become, how shrunken ourselves in relation to the great negatives that stood massive around us, taller, more oppressive than our hills. There was nothing we could do save march in single, penitential file chewing our softer cinders in suits of dark sackcloth to the officials of the Exchange and the Assistance Board. To them we would make obeisance, kiss the stamp upon our cards as a token of submission and stand still to have our heads shriven in order to cool the thoughts within that still had enough of human passion to tempt us into taking steps to establish on a surer footing the happiness of a fellow being. We felt some regret as we thought of Eurona lying on that bed with Morris crouched on the landing peering in at her with his special brand of blank dismay which was very blank indeed.

The sense of having failed made us itch. We made excuses into our own minds where the fact of failure lounged about in its native shadow and laughed at us. Perhaps, in Eurona, we had chosen the wrong vehicle for our trial trip in effective interference with the lives of others. Perhaps, tolerated misery had now cut such teeth as to be biting great potholes in the road we trod to trip us headlong every time we ventured to take a step that lacked the previous sanction of the organised trappers who directed our living and waited for the spring to snap that would let them have our fur at the lowest rates. Or the feebleness of our gesture in our tiny conflict with authority and foolishness showed a slowing down, a dying of our very ability to act as if alive and send rockets of defiance tearing through the darkening humiliation of our state.

My friend Ben would not take this last view. We were as alive as ever, he said. He thumped his fist on the bricks of the wall we sat on as he said that. As alive as ever. The phrase sounded good and we asked him to repeat it. He did and added that it was Eurona who had put our efforts in the ditch, no one else. She was modelled on her old man, a block off the old block, doomed to become a grey, scared shudder with a higher vibration even than Morris. When she really completed her cycle as premier victim of the life force in the seven stone class she and Morris would have attained a pitch of sensitive terror in the face of the capers that beset them; they would twang like a pair of harps every time they stuck their heads out of doors and prepared to fight their way towards another evening.

'And the cause of it all,' said my friend Arthur taking over the torch of protest from Ben, 'is this love. Not even as warmth should it be put up with any longer. There will be no peace, no dropping of the present gale, until we go around with banners running down this love and demanding some other way for the voters to pass on the time when they are not at work or in gaol or too old. It sits at the bottom of our brains eating away all sense and purpose like a mad rat. We could have done more with a badger or a beaver than we have done with this Eurona. At least we could have got the beaver off to that foxhunter and by now it would have been dusting the shorter articles such as the hunter's boots and telling the foxes of conditions here in the Terraces and giving pleasure to the Ministry of Labour which stands for labour and likes to see it going on even though it never gets more than a foot from the ground.

'That Rollo! That's a bright beauty to go sticking the heart out at. We should have boiled Eurona's mind before we took to agitating on her behalf so it would not have turned sour and thick on her first night of great emotion. We should have let Morris get hold of that mauve suit he fancied. The boys at the Exchange would have given him a card to match. A mauve card. That's the one they give you when you've used up more than your fair quota of ink and floor board and they introduce you to the other worms in the boring department and they fit you in cosily behind the woodwork. At least Morris would have given us no trouble with such foolishness as falling in love. He's so flattened out he's got nowhere to fall from unless he is hoisted up specially for the job. If he has all those kids that is only because he is full of those genes that are pedalling backwards to get away from Morris. Down with love, I say. It has put more wits on the loll than tyranny, hunger, dodging the rent man or death. Let us be like dogs. If the business must go on, don't let's drag personalities into it. Sniff and pass on. We'll all do a session of hard steady sniffing tomorrow to get the Terraces used to the notion. And all we'll need then for fair subsistence will be a spare nose and a hard biscuit. And no believers coming around threatening us with an immortality of this. Dogs, for those voters, are outside the gate.'

We agreed. We would not all be as bitter as Arthur but he had the disadvantage of having started out with more hope than we. Arthur was still moved by the charming geometrical myths that stress an ultimate concordance of desire, medium and fulfillment. We discussed the business a little further. We decided we would apologise to the Government for all the trouble we had put them to, make some restitution on the lines of a penny a month for the next hundred years and issue a public recantation of our previous views on political economy which no longer held water if the brains of all the poorer subjects turned out to be as leaky as Eurona's. At the same time, we would ask Ben's wife, a noted needlewoman, to stitch together, from any fragment of blue and yellow material she might find on the flagstaff and in old family chests, a few garments similar in cut and colour to those that had so beguiled Rollo and were now ash. We also agreed that as a dessert to these proceedings we would take a stand on some well covered roof beneath which Rollo was bound to pass on his way to the valley, give it a good shake and bring a few tiles pelting down on Rollo's head. After that, we felt, we should have to leave Eurona and her great load of unreason and grief to the dusty quiet of her loneliness.

*****

But on the very day following that discussion we and Eurona's problem slipped into the life stream of Shadrach Sims, a man of deep, strange significance.

The four of us received printed cards early in the morning telling us that the manager of the Exchange would be pleased to see us. In the type of lives we led at that period, reduced to the frigid bareness of food, roof, breath, we had little occasion to meet and enjoy these paper flowers of urbanity. They give a lovely purple glow to living, these smooth, gentle courtesies. But to our unused ears they have a brilliancy that churns up and gives us a quick choice between laughter and weeping. Even we would not be pleased to see us. Yet here was this manager, a man puissant, lofty and secure, saying it. It was satisfying. When a few minutes' thought had misted over the bloom of a lying culture, we wondered what this interview could be for. Our age group and temperament put us out of the running for any of the light industrial jobs that were being created under pressure from above in our own and the surrounding valleys. If men of our kind set out to do all the keen-eyed jostling required to get one of those positions we would be so tired after the getting we would spend the first year of employment resting in a quiet doze on the job. In any case these openings were kept for adolescents who needed more encouragement to live than we, not yet having got incurably into the habit, and if anyone were to mistake such grizzled and pensive applicants as ourselves for adolescents that man would need to have poor sight or an even poorer vocabulary.

Nor would the manager have asked to see us for a general chat. We had already discussed the social problem with him at such length we had now reached the curve in sense and were making our way by the same route as we had come, back to silence. The walls of his office were dented by our head marks where we had banged the record of our despair and our wish to be done with the blank, ugly fissure that separated his conclusions from our own. It struck us too, that the interview might be about Eurona. This made us sad and wary. We had acted in good faith. But our good faith was as something that is spoken of by men with wandering eye and tongue from a far land. It was taken with so much salt it felt like a chip. The Government did not see the point of being deceived in its own country. It reserved the right to work off on us, we not being busy at anything else, the spleen it might feel at being fooled about outside its own boundaries. We were the raw material of a shrewd governmental mood, no more. The details of this Eurona issue would provide them with material for some pretty blows. Criminal folly was the least of the cherries they could put atop our cake. We had gone the rounds of two Government Departments and the big hearts of the New Age Group, lying like a pack of clowns and soiling the good name of the working people. We had deceived the foxhunter who had been told to expect Eurona on a given day and he was probably sitting even now in undusted dignity in that Peace of which he was a Justice, wondering whether he could set his hounds on us without spoiling their power of scent. Or they might think the sight of us bitten half to death by the JP's dogs an anti-climax and they would strap us to Mount Snowdon to be pecked raw by flights of winged solicitors, all sharply clawed to winkle out the eyes of those who edged too overtly close to the eyries of the rich and mad for the flavour of compressed torment that made such a delicacy of our improvident kidneys...

We made our way down the hill that led to the valley bed. Whatever the aim and end of the interview it was good to have it to think about. We had got to the stage where there was no longer any programme of serious intention in our fear. We created dreads in our imagination simply to see if we could uncover some new specimen whose markings were different from those we knew already. We had nowhere to run to even had fear been active and no belief that we could ever prevent the object of our fear, more knowing and swifter than we, from doubling back and facing us even as we ran. We had lost the urge to run. Our breath had grown shorter than our finger nails and was nowhere near as pointed or useful. Ben, whose thoughts were always dramatic and called up prospects of gaol as easily as those of others lust or food, took a sombre view. According to him we would not be forgiven for introducing the sand of a good intention into the frugal ethics of the administration. We had tried to act like fairy godmothers, and people with patched trousers and no connection with bankers save human shape do not do so well in that part. Our falseness would be given some special mark of degradation, to adorn our breach of that brute inertia in which we were called upon to reside. They would strike for us a croix de guerre of a novel kind, a double croix of the social guerre, reserved for those who had been stripped of all except truth and were now found to be thrusting even that into the ash-can.

'Whatever that manager says to us,' said Ben as we came to the foot of the Terraces, 'there's one way we could always atone.'

'How?' asked Arthur cautiously. He always thought twice or not at all about Ben's suggestions. To Arthur with his oddly cool grey eyes and his mind weaving an unrelenting wisdom from its communion of sleepless hatred with his disordered stomach there was always something shocking about the belief, simple, pervasive as dew, that Ben held in solving every problem by an assertion of sheer bodily resistance. At that moment, we could see

69

that Arthur expected Ben to suggest that as soon as we got to the Exchange we should enter the manager's office, tear up a floor board and then put the floor board back, on top of the manager.

'How?' asked Arthur again.

'We could use Morris.'

'I can't see,' said our friend Walter, looking up into Ben's big, dark, convinced face, 'how Morris is going to help us here. The Board won't believe he had anything to do with those negotiations about Eurona. Morris has never got far enough into life to argue the toss with anybody. He falls down and shouts "Allah" every time he sees anyone who looks like a Government official. Morris is God's gift to a worried Civil Service.'

'I wasn't exactly thinking of putting the blame on him,' said Ben. 'But we could say that Morris has now thought over this whole question of Eurona and how it disgraces his record in the matter of obeying all rules drawn up to keep us on all fours. He has decided therefore to make amends. He will give himself up and offer to provide the central clinker at a real old-fashioned festival. He will offer himself to be publicly burned as a new style heretic, as a double protest against the clumsy antics of Eurona and a final gesture against the frost that has been closing down upon him ever since he got really big enough for things to grip him squarely between thumb and forefinger.'

'It wouldn't do,' said Walter. 'That Morris, in addition to his other failings, would make the worst bit of firewood ever seen in these Terraces. The rain has soaked right through that man. He stands motionless like a small hill.

Whatever's raining, it can't miss Morris. You've heard of a man being half soaked. Well, Morris starts from there and if you ever see him leaving the ground without being lifted or shoved it will not be any miracle. It will be his bones, drenched with endured sorrows to the core, beginning to float. If we do have people starting up stakes and pyres in this division to uproot such things as disobedience and thought, to give them Morris would be the shortest way of teaching them sense. That man would never catch. It is years since Morris lost the last fragment of whatever it is in a man that gives forth flame.'

As we entered the Exchange we received courteous nods from the clerks. We always walked about with such a look of mature understanding it would not have surprised these clerks suddenly to find that a huge beacon of insight had been set off in our brains and that we had now beaten the whole problem of want among men. They wanted to be sure that when that day came, we would make them some return for the years of patient sympathy which had, no doubt, done much to make our thought a tool of such cutting edge, so cutting it is now used to open everything except the thicker tins. As we walked the length of the big hall towards the manager's office we were grotesquely straight in face and body. Partly, it was due to the gauntness of the hall designed by some body of genuine artists in depression to strip the average voter of hope and cheer twice as fast as Dante's fancy. Partly it was the thought of Eurona. There was nothing distinctively tragic in the failure of her schemes and her present plight. She was a fair specimen of that woeful daftness that spoils all dignity and negates all

71

purpose in a community whose intimate traditions and self-conceits had taken a thorough shellacking, a gripless fatuity of mental action that undermines the whole system of interlocking relevancies and reduces the equipment of social existence to a dangerous and chilling fragility. There was nothing special about the destiny of Eurona that would make us want to call upon Jenkins the Harpist to accompany us in a richly harmonised rendering of 'All Through the Night' with Twentieth-Century Amendments. But in her flimsy silliness, in her utter lack of defences, the morbid completeness of her present grief, laboured to a high finish as if someone were being paid time-and-a-half for filling in the details, she was a token of all the deprivation we were learning to take in doses that grew larger and, with the merciful numbing of the gullet, less bitter with the passing of each day. Viewed in relation to her father, a man whose consistency of grey apathy would have made him life's favourite spittoon if he had only been flatter, rounder and noticeably hollow, she was, as we heard that man say in the lecture down at the Library and Institute, the negation of the negation. Two blacks making another black, as their way is. The thought of her pressed upon the dull broad back of our brain, heightening the awareness of the sensitive, painful forefront.

Mr Simpson, the manager, sat in his office waiting for us. He had the usual mountain of papers and pens in front of him as if he were only awaiting the nod that would show the world to be willing before he began to change it right and left. He gave us friendly greeting. We gave a like greeting to him. We bowed reverently to a picture of a man framed and

72

hanging on the wall above Mr Simpson's head. This was a man who had walked into that Exchange eight years before and got work right away. Since then we had him unofficially canonised and each New Year's Eve we took a vow that when we emerged from the monsoon we could club in and hang a floral tribute on the frame of his portrait.

The manager looked pleased, even coy. This meant that Eurona was not on the agenda and our stiffness relaxed.

'You are not such bad chaps,' he said. 'There's something not bad at all about you four. Yes, you've got your heads screwed on the right way. Yes, you've got your heads screwed on all right.'

He put a lot of emphasis on that as if he were really glad that we were now doing this screwing and not keeping our heads loose and rattling and liable to be left behind and lost when we left the building. We were pleased to hear this praise. Praise is the only true recognition of life and there are many who get so little of this recognition they take themselves for dead twenty or thirty years before their time which is confusing to their relatives who are often not told a word about these inner burials. If we heard praise coming at us from a small hole in the wainscoting, we would bend down and beam back our gratitude and tell the shadows and the mice that we would willingly do as much for them every time they feel depressed about being down so low. At the same time we were not fully at ease on hearing those words from Mr Simpson. For all we knew, Mr Simpson might well go on to say that the Government, having watched the flowering of our ability with keen interest, was no longer willing to humiliate us with the weekly offering of a dole and would we please shift off the Insurance and make way for a quartet of elements younger, stronger, whose fingers would be less itchy with the tingle to go probing into the knot of shadows where knowing, pity and desire hang like soft, dark petals, waiting for us to pluck them off and have some part and pride in the tale of our own eclipse and mutilation.

'Have you heard of Shadrach Sims?' asked Mr Simpson.

Of course we had heard of Shadrach Sims. The only people who had never heard of Shadrach Sims are people who have either given up eating or eat only things that are free like grass or paper without print. This Sims had a chain of small grocery shops running up and down the valley which soon became a chain of large ones running in the same direction. He also owned two big stores where clothes and furniture were sold and much liked by people who still dressed and sat down. He also had the Pontine Palace, the cinema in the bottom terrace near the bridge where such stupefying programmes were shown to the tightly packed patrons you could walk to your seat from any part of the building and not touch the floor. You could tread on nothing but human heads and hear not a word of complaint for the subjects who went regularly to the Pontine, between the injections of pictorial poppy from the screen and queuing up at the ventilators trying to remember whose turn it is to breathe next, have skulls that have been done hard like eight-minute eggs but would be disowned on grounds of sub-standard flavour and food value by any chicken. The name of Shadrach Sims had taken on among us a note of fable. In a place where practically everything except houses, public conveniences and mouths had closed down, where even the mountains looked down with contempt and seemed to stay only because they were too busy to be clomping around looking for a fresh patch to get rooted in and blither beings than we to people their flanks, this man Shadrach was the chief of those who had broken free from the ruck of failure. He was one of the very few who had appeared to order life as we used to order suits, choose the wanted fabric from a book of samples, pick the cut from a book of styles and have it let out at the fork if the sun became too sweltering and the fit too tight. Mothers sitting in the dark because their kids had just run off with the last gas penny and spent it drib drab on such articles as liquorice, bobby dazzlers and single pages of old comics, spoke to these kids of Shadrach Sims who probably had his own gas works in the back, tossed in a match from time to time and read and went about his other business by the light of the explosions. Women who cut down grandparents' garments for the use of their children and then had to cut down the grandparents to find some use for the garments because the kids preferred to go about in decent nakedness, spoke of Shadrach Sims who wore so many suits at once he could not move for sheer weight of cloth and had to be carried from bank to bank. More, this Shadrach Sims had been born in the Terraces, had even spent some time as a pupil in the same primary school as we had attended. He saw little point in the instruction he had got there, detected swiftly, we had no doubt, that this type of schooling was a botched compromise between slavery and freedom, meant to confuse the naturally lucid and make timid the naturally bold. He ran away early to master the grocery trade in different parts of Britain, opening up new lines of guile and sharp practice that caused veteran colleagues to have their own relative honesty written up and illustrated in a series of homely sketches in stained glass. By the age of forty Shadrach had become the valley's premier grocer. He organised Food Clubs which placed a layer of solid magic on the lives of the very needy. A group of families would club in a shilling a week for twenty weeks and then in turn each family would receive a pound's worth of groceries all at once, always including some little delicacies normally unbought but yearned for in a thousand hungry dreams. This is not to say that these people did no eating at all in between the weeks on which they received Shadrach's momentous hampers, but after the splendour of that assembled pound's worth, the hard tack that was their normal due got little more from them than a nerveless nibble, keeping up the required quota of iron in their diet by taking an occasional bite direct from the hob. So many of these people went light in the head or down flat in a faint at the sight of some particular titbit in the basket, a First Aid man always went along with the vanboy to jerk them up or give them something to sniff at and scatter earth on their ecstasy. Another feature worth noting about Shadrach was that he had nothing to do with the chapels. Men who did well out of trade in the valley were quick to extol their own piety and affirmed their own dependence on prayer as if without it they could not be relied upon to keep even their trousers up. When they reached a certain figure at the bank they thought this to be a singular mark of godliness and often broke away from their chapel and set up a new one where their central place in the deacons' seat and a strong grip on the preacher's neck would put their identification with Yaweh beyond any of the doubt that had sometimes harassed them in the old establishment. These rich traders, like everybody else in the Terraces and outside, were trying to say something about themselves and the chapels were the handiest chisels they could find to cut out the words of their message on the skulls of their fellows. But there was nothing of the sort about Shadrach. If he had ever prayed his way out of the shadows he had taken some of the shadow with him to wrap around the fact for we had not heard of it. He might have been a Turk giving away free fezzes to the organisers of his Food Clubs for all the interest he took in anything but shops, money and turning out new brands of cretin from the Death-to-Thought-and-Go-Outside-to-Do-It League that met nightly at the Pontine Palace. For several years past, Shadrach had lived in a renovated mansion in a wooded valley in the rich countryside to the west of us. We had heard little of him save that he was lavish in the study and sensual expression of his appetites.

'Of course we've heard of him,' said my friend Walter. 'Anybody with as much money, food and clothes as Sims could carve a kingdom out of these Terraces if he didn't mind the thing being a little bony.'

'He's come back here.'

'Here? What for? He's got a mansion. A mansion in a Carmarthenshire valley that's deep, full of trees and like a song.'

'Know it. I've seen it. That's the place to live, boy. Serene. Two acres of lawn and flowers sloping down to a river that's clean. That's the only place to live.'

'We'll think it over,' said Arthur. 'But what about Shadrach?'

'He's come back here because he's worried by the competition of the other chain stores that have been setting up chains here. So he's planning a big advertising campaign to remind the people that Sims is still first and best.'

'Good luck to him. We like to see men like Sims believing in themselves like that. It gives us boys a bit of margin in which to wonder whether we're even here or not. But what's this to do with us?'

'He wants four men to do the rough work, the odd jobs of the campaign in this lower part of the valley.'

'You mean,' said Walter in a deep hostile voice, staring at the portrait of our patron saint, the first timer, on the wall, 'you mean you want us to march about with slogans praising Sims, slogans on boards, sandwich men?'

'What about it?' asked Mr Simpson. 'What's wrong with being a sandwich man? An honest calling. What's wrong with it?'

'That's a daft question, Mr Simpson. For a long time we've been asking what's wrong with being just a man, seeing the horses doing so much better than we do. But nobody answers. For fifteen years, off and on, mostly on, we've been losing hope, health, hair, teeth and, in one of the hard winters yet to come, toes as well so we won't even be able to kick the people we can't bite now. But we've been developing dignity on a broad front. We may not be very much to look at but we've put a lot of serious thought into the shapes and expressions we have at present. We don't want to walk about with these shapes cloaked in boards. We want all the local children to have a good clean view of us because we are among the few object lessons they will ever see that are willing to come forward and sing their own foot notes. If we look so much like high class ghouls the Council put double locks on the graveyard gate we want people to see all the details that drove the Council to this step. When we are cloaked in boards we shall be lying down flat, enjoying every minute of it, and the boards, unless our relatives decide to make a bit extra by letting the plain wooden surfaces be used for advertising during the short trip to the Black Meadow where they bury us boys, will not have a word about Shadrach Sims on them. Sandwich men ought to be where they belong, on South Sea Islands, being eaten.'

'Don't be so touchy. There'll be all sorts of jobs. I can't imagine anybody as smart as Shadrach Sims using a trick as old as the sandwich board. There'll be handbills to give out and stick up. It's a good opening.'

'Into what?'

'Into the giving out and sticking up trades. Shadrach told me to make sure that the men I chose could read from left to right, big print and small, and be able to explain by word of mouth why Sims is still the first and best. I thought of you four straightaway. You've been running that political discussion group up in the Terraces for eighteen years now showing why capitalism and practically everything else is doomed, which shows you can explain things. Most of the people in the Terraces, after listening to you in the evening, are so amazed to wake up in the morning and find capitalism still there, they wait for the thing to come around in the afternoon and say it's sorry. So it'll be a nice change for you to talk about Sims and the grocery trade instead. There are not many things you believe in but I can see from your looks that you believe in food, so you are not likely to go about proving that groceries are doomed.'

We listened with interest. We had never heard Mr Simpson in this clowning vein before. We smiled at him in encouragement. We thought it good that the Government should adopt a touch of smiling fancy in its dealings with the poorer voters. It might lead them to take a light view of such things as Eurona dumping Government gifts on to the fire while impudently remaining unburnt herself.

'And the pay,' added Mr Simpson, 'will be three pounds a week.'

'Good God,' we said. After a decade and a half in the economic cellarage this was like being hoisted out on the end of a crane. That sum per week seemed to put us ahead even of a man like Sims.

'He'll want to see you this afternoon.'

'He'll want to make sure that we can still move. That's only fair. Where?'

'He's living in a flat above his main shop.'

'All right then. Give us the green cards.' These were the cards one had to have when consulting a possible employer to prove to him that you were alive and legal. Without the card, even if you capered in front of the employer giving over a whole hour to solo singing and handsprings, you would still be, administratively, a corpse, waiting for its shroud of white cards. We have known dying voters holding up the business and hanging on for years, afraid to take any serious step in the matter of breath without the stamped permission of the proper authorities who had got the psyche of these voters on a strong lead after years of interviews, warnings and hints.

On our way back to the Terraces, we thought over our talk with Mr Simpson, staring at the green cards in our hands as if we were scholars and they a codex of unfathomable value. We were in a yes and no mood. We had not yet decided that Sims was the alley way we needed. We had grown accustomed to the static and waited for a suggestion that would blow our minds firmly in this direction or that.

'I'm for passing these cards on to the dog,' said Arthur. 'I have no love for this Shadrach Sims. And between my stomach and the world crisis I have so little to do with his groceries I don't want to go about the streets putting him and them forth as a kind of gospel.'

'That's right,' said Ben. 'It'll be a false move, I'll venture. After a week of trying to get Shadrach crowned the first and the best, God knows what we'll be up to next. We might even be volunteering to collect rents for the landlords, wheedling the tenants into arrears just for the pleasure of putting them on to the pavement and fanning the families of the landlords during the dog days. Evil is like hair. It grows on you.'

'No,' said our friend Walter. 'We'll go and see Shadrach. He's an unusual man. Anybody who can wring a mansion out of the Terraces and still have the reputation of being pagan is worth watching. In any case it doesn't make much difference what we do. And if we earn a little extra we may

81

be able to square this matter of Eurona. We can pay back the Board and the New Agers, restore their faith in the word of the local supplicants and send Eurona to the Home Counties away from the blighting touch of Morris and Rollo as soon as the Vacancies Counter tells us that the hunter has a vacancy for a human tremor to run up and down the spine of his foxes.'

*****

That afternoon, we climbed the stairs that led to the apartment of Shadrach Sims. We heard his voice telling us to enter when we knocked. We filed in and stood by the door. He was sitting in a leather arm chair, smoking a cigarette. He was a man in his late forties, with hair on its way to grey, a blue suit and a red-lined, good-looking face, like the faces you see on those advertisements where men chosen for their look of power and success tell you they are now working twice as hard and earning twice as much since they heard of the firm to which they are now renting their faces. His was the face of a man so thoroughly self-knowing and in possession of himself as to seem almost unbelievable to us from whose idiom the imperatives of having and holding had been rubbed away. We too appeared to be unbelievable to Shadrach for he stared at us for a full half minute, his lower lip hanging down in an astonished droop.

'Jesus Christ,' he said.

We turned around, thinking we had company.

'What's the matter?' asked Walter.

'What the hell is this valley doing for people?' asked

Shadrach in a quiet, disgusted voice. 'I've been out of it for a good few years. I come back. All the joy seems to have died out of it. It's like a graveyard. And all because a few damned pits close down. It's not good enough. Makes a man sick and frightened to see it. Life shouldn't be like that, changing colour quickly like a face. There's something more than being short of money at the bottom of this. Any fool can get over a little thing like being short of money.'

He stared at us again and walked around us as if planning to buy us if we would knock the price down. We showed him the corner of our green cards to indicate that that might be arranged. It was clear that Shadrach was concerned and wished in his quick, efficient way to do something about us. For our part we were beginning to look upon him as five feet eight of miracle, no less, a weaver of the most amazing myths we had ever heard and with enough money to believe them, which makes all the difference to a myth. We know, for we have had in our brief and queer time to abandon many a fine substitute for truth for lack of the few extra shillings that are needed to keep an outsize lie clothed and fed to the point of fitness required for a running fight with reason. To hear such views as these of Shadrach on the economic question made it easy to believe that Shadrach had spent eight years in a mansion in the country alone with a clear river, his appetites and the hired agents of their fulfilment. If he had spent them well under water wrapping seaweed as a breakfast food for people who were sprouting gills for lack of anything better to do, he would not have had an odder approach to this matter of how to keep alive when only half so.

'It's thinking that kills,' said Shadrach. 'Thinking and the rain and the shadow that come down from these hills. Look at your faces. They are... they are dark. What kind of thinking do you do that puts out the lights like that? What kind of a night are you chaps walking in?'

'We have mixed thoughts,' said Walter.

'That's it. Mixed-up, too, I bet. I can smell your sort of thoughts from here. The damp rotten smell you get in dingles and old woods. Daft thoughts about men being equal and having an easy life. Who's going to make it easy? Let me tell you something. I read a book once. I keep it on the table at the side of my bed. It helps me to keep all foolishness at arm's length. In this book it says that all life is a matter of Creative Will. You get a pile of days, dreams, energy and other people. We all get that pile to start off with. Even you, believe it or not. Either you end sitting on top of the pile patting it into the shape you want or you become part of it and smother. You blokes look smothered to me. The wrong notions have been making a heavy meal of your Creative Will and the same thing's been going on right through this valley. It's wrong and I'm the man to put it right. Pit labour, hymns and shadow, that's a healthy dish for you. No wonder we have eighty thousand people between these hills looking like a parade of phantoms. If you ever feel a twitch between your ears that's your mind hiccoughing over a tough fragment of the Creative Will. You're developing into woodlice, the lot of you. Seen wood-lice? Slow, grey and horrible. If somebody doesn't let some light and life into you, you'll be rotting away the last plank that keeps the national structure from toppling.'

84

Shadrach went to a huge walnut sideboard that stood at the further end of the room. He finished off a small glass of whisky that stood there, walked restlessly to the window to look out at the great rise of mountain ahead with its thin crown of dwarfed trees sloping timorously away from the sea winds. The trees must have reminded him of us for he gasped again disgustedly. Then he returned to the sideboard and stared full at himself in the mirror above it. His expression changed. He looked frankly delighted with himself.

It was now our turn to look astonished. We could not imagine such ideas coming from a human head without an explosion of after-damp that would lift off part of the scalp. But there was not a ripple of the skin beneath Shadrach's hair. He had obviously been coaching his head in the art of reacting with calm to the terrible fermentation of dead reason and refusing to budge. We stood silent, Ben, Arthur, and I, expecting from our friend Walter a ringing oration that would prove to the satisfaction of everyone in that room except Shadrach that Shadrach was a maniac. We thought that not merely because he insulted groups of people like ourselves who had less power than he through the accident of not having the same urge to be gathering coins but because his kind of mania was even then leading our less assertive brethren in all the continents of the world through a long curriculum of misery and terror. We had heard with interest what Shadrach had said about the Creative Will. We were interested in anything that did not require a licence or rent. We had known a lot of people in the Terraces full to the very brim with this very article and slopping over with the impulse to be at grips with the world and increase their savings, security or simply their own sense of individual identity. They had set forth of a morning with a whole armful of Creative Will only to get as far as the back door, to be questioned sharply and hit silly, having the Will or the back door cracked over their heads by one or other of those shrewd fellows whose job it is to see that the act of creation, in a social sense, should be limited to the old, narrow and familiar channels of yesteryear. True, we were all given at birth a pile of days, dreams and so on through the catalogue as given out by Shadrach. But there are some whose hands are gentler and slower to move on their own behalf, tethered at every moment and in every act by a pity as savage in its compulsion as any hatred, haunted by an impression of life as a thing rocking with bewilderment from age to age and wearing on its face a look of terrified sorrow. We had projected from ourselves into things and people a myth of absolute sensitiveness that had brought us to a mood of staring, wary immobility by implanting in us an unsleeping fear of doing the same kind of hurt to others as we endured. We had addressed ourselves to the evolution of a profound and automatic sympathy as thoroughly as Shadrach to the garnering of shops and profit. We had lived to further a process of thought and feeling whose aim was to note and make known the roots and operations of distress among men. From that, to cause in men a shame and anger that would lead them to question the rightness of those who found some consolation in having in our midst great reservoirs of need, obscurity and fear. In our way we had attained almost to the same high level of bounding sufficiency as Shadrach but our aims were still darkling and lacked the golden opinions won by his. He travelled in a medium whose ideas, resting on a contemptuous refusal to look beneath the avoidable indignities and filth of those whose beings bend, stammer and serve only to fertilise the age's crop of greatness, were tiny, uncomplicated and granted the traveller unhindered speed and power over a human landscape that was simple and smooth with the cement laid down to cheat the soil beneath of new, confusing change and growth. We were seeking, without wealth, influence or a map, for the materials of a new social understanding aimed at something lower than love, a muddied concept, but fixed beyond the chilling reach of envy and contempt. A large order as all know who have taken more than half a dozen steps beyond the cradle. Now here was this Shadrach measuring our rhapsody for the hatchet and describing us as woodlice. We gave the term some thought for we had never been called that in the afternoon before. We are larger, fairer-skinned and faster. We eat no wood unless it has been thoroughly ground beforehand. As for nibbling the last plank of the national structure, we live in such shadow we are never sure unless supplied in advance with a torch what we are nibbling and I have already explained about our teeth. They are fragile and cadent. Creative Will... There would be many in the Terraces who would take those words to be Christian names and wonder whether Creative had any relatives living in those parts. I could see the fingers of my friend Ben closing and opening, punctuating some great sentence of wrath.

'You're right, Mr Sims,' said Walter, breaking a silence we had not understood. 'We are just what you say. You're a lighthouse. You have insight. You see through us. We are they that have grown in darkness and that should never be said of men who are never sought after at dawn like mushrooms, and are without scarcity value. You to us are a man with sight compared with men who have no eyes. The Creative Will is dying in all of us who have witnessed the decline of life between these mountains. Morton the Undertaker has his ear cocked for the last gasp and his thumb up for a rough measurement. When he has done, one of these hills that box us in will be the greatest tumulus of unused creative ability ever to show its jesting bulge to men. The great urge to get on, to make something of ourselves, of the gifts that lie within us all, is falling to sleep to a lullaby of squalid desperation. We have been left too much alone, Mr Sims. We need the sight and sound of men like you to make the blood of our lives run warm and inquiring again. Initiative has slipped so swiftly and in such bulk into the drains we have detachments of scouts stationed at every culvert to catch what bits of it can still be restored. A new Yoga, shorn of all aim and method is falling like a vapour on the voters and there are some who have reached a stage in their war against expression where they even have to be lured into the toilet with subterfuge, birdcalls and offers of rewards. We await our resurrection, Mr Sims. You are the man.'

'Yes, yes,' said Shadrach. We admired the utter lack of any need to doubt and question in this Shadrach. He probably sent letters of congratulation to himself every morning. The last strange words of our friend Walter were coursing through him like wine. He helped the wine on by going to the sideboard for another drink of whisky, and another session of busy adulation before the mirror. He came back to the table.

'Yes, yes,' he said again. 'You're right. I have the brain, the means, the faith in strong selfish action that will banish the poison of complacent wretchedness. But I have no time. I want an agent, a man who will be an exact symbol of my standards, a mouth for the utterance of all my meditations. Where to find such a man in a place like this?'

He gave us another searching glance. We were shamefaced. We felt equal to a little bill distributing and, even, given a friendly brand of glue and a broad brush, a little bill sticking. But we could go no part of the way to answering Shadrach's ideal. Looking at us, you could think of a lot of things, even human beings, but never of Creative Will. In any case, as far as Shadrach's requirements went there was nothing on our green cards to say that we were fit or able to take up such jobs as symbolising or uttering and that ruled us out. We always went by the card.

'There's a lad up in the Terraces,' said Walter, 'who would fill your bill to the T. His name is Rollo Watts. He is pretty. The maidens treat him as a god and line his path in a ten-foot layer. He has a fine direct faith in getting on. He has given up thought save on such simple issues as remembering his name and the date. He is so full of the Creative Will it keeps his hair sticking up, slops over and has to be swept up every time he bends. He is known to be an enemy of all this nonsense about equality and looks upon us all with a scorn that is bracing and antiseptic. This scorn would do us the world of good if we were not so far gone. He also has a job,

89

a uniform to do it in, and golfing knickers to keep himself in the public eye when he is not doing the job. He has a young friend too, a widow from London whose late husband led a revolt against mercy and delusions of brotherhood in that area. These two, properly trained and encouraged, would give the stricken youth of this region a new point of departure, giving them the means of leaving the lakeside by boat instead of just jumping in as before.'

'That will be done,' said Shadrach. 'A little free food here, a few free cinema shows there and we'll have those two at the head of a movement that will, within a year, banish the sickly fumes of this mouldering mania to be weak, meek and scabrous, to be levelling us all to the common flatness of the mud at the river's bed.' Shadrach's face grew pale as he said that. The mud of the black slow river that flowed through our view seemed to fill him with a special horror. 'Send those two young people to me. I'll have a chat with them, sound them, see how far they can follow my notions and put flesh around them, the thick deathproof flesh that the young love.' He repeated the words thick and young, as if regretting that our taste in flesh ran so obviously to thin, threadbare stuff, stretched in the tension of accepted mortality, proof only against desire, opening its pores on birthdays and Maydays for a quick whiff of the world and only then. Shadrach made another trip to the bottle on the sideboard. With his glass at his lips he said again: 'I'll sound them. Yes, I can see it now, as clear as day, I can see it now.'

We craned our heads but could see nothing but Shadrach. He noticed the gesture and made haste to admit us to the view.

'I see a fine strong virile movement of marching boys and girls, with headquarters at the Pontine Palace where they will see wholesome films. I can see them marching and countermarching, damning the spineless capers of communal and co-operative effort, burning the beds of the loungers who breed but do not toil and working up such a hunger in their guts with all these parades their grocery bills will go up a hundred per cent. Trade and their hearts will revive in the same glorious breath.'

'I'll bring them to you,' said Walter in a curious, flat and satisfied voice.

Then Shadrach told us of the job we were to do, described the area to be covered, the type and number of the bills to be given out and stuck up, the quality of the verbal propaganda to be retailed to those who were slow to believe the printed statements about Sims, or liked things better said than read. When he had finished he sat down once more to smoke. His complacency, between the whisky and the way we stood there dumbly listening, had reached a fresh peak. His face looked the cosiest thing on earth. With leather binding on the ears to take the strain one could have sat on it and felt grateful. He glanced at us with one eye half closed, amused.

'To think,' he said. 'You four and me were at the same school at the same time.'

We did not grasp the exact implication of that. But from the broad excited grin on Shadrach's face we could see that the implication was tickling him most pleasantly. He was thinking perhaps of the irony that made one institution, a school in this instance, a pen for animals so manifestly different in function and end as tigers and goats. We knew what team we belonged to and we felt sorry, especially when faced by such well made men as Shadrach that the law no longer allowed us even the old-fashioned privilege of working off an odd butt here and there. 'Remember the time I chased the teacher, that woman teacher?' he asked.

He put his head back and laughed. We all smiled and said we did, as if our memories were still chuckling at the vision of that rare frolic. But we remembered nothing of Shadrach's schooldays in any detail. He may for all we knew have bought himself out of his surplus savings a whole set of hand-made memories equipped with everything but truth but with the power to give warmth to his thoughts of days whose reality still shivered in his imagination. We wondered what he had wanted from that teacher that made him willing to run for it, what kind of a race she had put up and what she had felt like when she found her breath getting shorter and Shadrach getting taller and closing in on her. Life, it seemed to us as we pondered the plight of that teacher and looked into the bright, brutal eyes of this rapacious and nimble-footed fellow, was not lacking in dramatic and horrible possibilities. 'Be here tomorrow morning,' he said when he had decided to give us no more memoirs for that day. We withdrew, raising our green cards twice in the ceremonial salute of departing applicants.

We made our way down the stairs. Once outside, we jumped on our friend Walter for an explanation of his motives in tolerating the chatter of Shadrach and adding to the general hail of folly some fancy brands of his own.

'Think,' said Walter. 'What would happen to Shadrach if

he went through the Terraces giving tongue to the crapulous doctrines we've just been putting up with?'

'I'd make a dent in his head that you could bathe in,' said Ben.

'Something more official and thoughtful than that.'

'You haven't seen the kind of dent I'm thinking of, Walter. It would be a blemmer. Down to the neck and with the sides all smooth so as not to annoy the birds that will drink from it.'

'No, Ben. That's just your selfish fancy. A dent of the kind you mean would improve Shadrach's head no end but I am thinking of something broader. What would the people do?'

'They'd take a few tons of Creative Will,' said Arthur, 'and make from it a maypole. From that maypole they would give Shadrach such a stretching he'd be only too glad to say so long and no longer.'

'And what would happen to that Rollo if Shadrach were to persuade him to go forth and act as Shadrach's apostle?'

'The same maypole, only shorter.'

*****

After tea, we went along to the house of Morris to see what was happening to Eurona. We had told no one of our interview with Shadrach. The sight of us going about as the hired workmen of Shadrach Sims was bound to cause a lot of excitement and remark. In the past years we had been well known as men who had stuck rigidly to the Insurance, except for one short spell shovelling snow from the streets, so short we felt sure the thaw had been told about us in advance. Some people in the Terraces even claimed that the Government paid us a small retaining fee to keep us giving a look of quiet dignity to the whole system of public relief. We thought it better therefore to let this news about Shadrach break upon our neighbours in the form of an accomplished thing. To herald it forth that evening as one of the morrow's miracles would cause a mood of reckless joy and mad celebration to run through the Terraces, bringing a light of painful brilliance into minds long adjusted to penumbra standard, driving neighbours to crowd around us and hail us as the first swallows of their greatest spring and demand that we begin there and then to chirp to put the matter beyond any doubt. We would sidle cautiously towards our new good fortune and let the thing get used to the sight of us before taking hold of it and stroking it to an accepting purr. It might yet snap at us and drive us back to chilly exile.

We found Morris alone in his kitchen. He was staring at the fire over which he was doubled as if the fire had done him some hurt. He seemed to be at rock bottom. He looked tired as if he had been trying his best to get down even deeper. But he had failed. Morris could go no further. He was there. He had arrived. From the stupefied stillness of his face and the defeated droop of his body we had an impression of feeling the breath of the rock on which he had now come to rest, cold. His mood was troubled and bitter and could be seen sticking out of him like a fretwork frame. He was moaning too, a favoured tactic with Morris whenever he thought people might be in doubt about the way he felt. He was ranked next as a moaner to my friend

Arthur's Aunt Ceridwen, the saddest woman in the Terraces, who kept alive on roasted cheese and the tale of disasters and went around the various vestries and halls of the valley doing short sketches about grief old and new which sent such a chill through the voters they would be found crouched in a terrible cramp beneath the benches or seen leaving the hall rubbing each others' limbs to keep the blood within a foot of either end of the body. But we always thought that Morris did not lag behind Aunt Ceridwen. There was a smoothness on the low notes and a neighing quality on the higher level that were always good to hear and even repaid any trouble you might take to goad him into a spasm with accounts of some fresh affliction that would shortly be making a target of his neck. He was on some special form that afternoon twisting his head in a way that made his voice slither through whole scales. Ben held his head still and pulled the chair he sat on away from the chimney place so that we could know for certain whether Morris were really moaning and not singing.

'How is Eurona?' asked Walter.

'I don't know and I don't care,' said Morris, giving Ben a push and putting his head into a spin that almost shook his eyes out. He grew calmer when he saw the serious look on all our faces. He felt that these defiant answers were not in place and that we wanted some sense from him even if we had to put him over a lemon squeezer and extract the truth from the gall that way. He told us Eurona was still lying on the bed upstairs, making no sign of ever wanting to join in life's march again and taking no food.

'No food at all,' he said. 'I'll tell you what she's doing.

She's trying to starve to death. Will they blame me for that?'

'No. She's doing it off her own bat. They won't give it a second thought unless they have photographs showing you driving Eurona away from the grub.'

'Nothing like that with me, Walter. If people can find the grub they're welcome.'

His face grew brighter as if he saw nothing wrong in this starving programme in itself. It was a big save in food and would rid him of a daughter who had turned his life into a solid block of problem by turning down jobs, burning clothes and giving the Government an idea that he was flippant in his dealings with them. Morris explained these things to us. We could see he had been thinking hard for several hours to have a crop of phrases like that bottled and ready for issue. He had struck a great vein of speech and he would have carried on talking in this way until the fire went down, we went out or the cold drove him aloft. So we told him, halfway through a long sentence that curled around him like a streamer that we had never heard a better statement than this on the current situation. Carved on old bones in pamphlet form with stiffened style and shorter groans and thrown through the windows of the mighty we could see it making a big difference, if only to the windows of the mighty. This judgement took him so much by surprise he fell silent, bewildered, and chewed upon this praise.

We asked his leave to go upstairs.

'A few words from us might do Eurona a bit of good,' said Walter.

96

Morris did not say no. Perhaps he may have objected to four grown-up people marching up his stairs without a writ from the County Council or a poked cap to show that we were going to inspect and condemn something. But he was in a lofty state after the long speech he had made on the folly of it all and the sincere praise he had received from us. He would not have objected to anything except perhaps to four grown-up voters marching through his kitchen carrying the stairs. We stood halfway up the stairs and began to call on Eurona. Morris by this time had come out of his trance. We could hear him muttering from the kitchen that in such a house as this with Eurona setting the pace in antisocial gestures it was no more to be expected that the climax should now be reached in the form of a whole chorus of voters blocking up his stairway doing a kind of Hallelujah chorus. The silence from the bedroom in which Eurona lay continued. Then my friend Arthur told her, in the gentlest voice, for God's sake, not to be so silly.

'Less of that,' said Morris in a savage whisper from the foot of the stairs. 'That's blasphemy. That's what they call that loose talk about God. I won't have it. We live rough but we draw the line there.'

Five minutes later, Eurona appeared at the head of the stairs. She looked a little shy and stunned but otherwise the same. She was dressed in her old clothes. To us who had last seen her in all that yellow splendour these clothes looked very old indeed. We felt as we stood there that we were taking part in some old-fashioned sketch. We all laughed, heavy, pealing laughter, as soon as we saw her, to show that we were glad to see her and saw nothing strange in the uncanny sag and drabness of her garments. Morris who was always startled out of his wits by laughter joined in until he saw it had no especial motive. Our laughter sounded loud and hollow in the narrow stairway as if it had no place there and bounced angrily away from walls which looked damp and dead. Morris raised a trembling arm and said that men who could stand on somebody else's stairs with no thought of going to bed and laugh in that manner were bound to be planning some mischief, bound to be a danger to quiet men like himself. He pressed his head into the discoloured crumbling woodwork as if seeking to wrap his thoughts around the fact of this new discomfort in handy hatchet form and lay them about our heads. When he began to speak he was too excited to be understood with ease but the upshot of it was that if this laughter of ours was the first stage in some new scheme to reclothe Eurona out of public funds, to warn him in advance so that he could give the campaign a hearty send off by trussing himself up into a neat parcel, with ourselves, he had no doubt, giving him a hand and making sure of the knots, and putting that on the fire. In that way he could be sure that he would be well out of it by the time Eurona got her next mad spell. As part of the ashes he would also avoid the shame of having to meet the sad, hurt reproachful eyes of those investigators and clerks down at the Assistance Board expressing disappointment with Morris on behalf of the Government.

We calmed him with the gift of a cigarette. We gave him, too, a promise that we would have the fire well stoked if he ever decided to put himself on it. We were all against the slow baking methods that were popular with the priests of long ago in their dealings with unbelievers. We told Eurona to follow us. She being stunned and still swept clean by grief of all critical reactions, love or hate, yes or no, what fun or what the hell, followed us without a word of question. Seeing her father standing behind us at the stair's bottom, rolling his eyes, shaking his head, making his way through a hundred moans of minor key to a record neigh that made him the horse's very best friend, a small grey monument to fear, might have made her glad to be one of our party and beyond the reach of his infectious dreads.

We took her to the house of my friend Ben. Ben's wife was a merry, kindly woman who would have done any number of good deeds a day if she had been able to afford them. She did a bit of spare time pie-baking for a bakery down in the valley. That day she had kept some of the meat pies which were her specialty back for her own use. Ben was a lover of those pies. He went so far as to say that these pies were the only things he ever thanked his father for when he and his father settled down to a serious talk on what Ben had gained from being born in the first place. When we walked into Ben's kitchen he said that although these pies were a kind of religion to him Eurona welcome to them if they would bring any gladness to her spirit. The craving of his own guts, ever a trade wind moulding the hillocks in the landscape of his soul, could go by the board.

'Ben,' said Walter, 'we have always known you for a comradely and considerate man, a help to the outcast, a friend of the spurned and a terror to the nark and the renegade. But your conduct in the matter of these delicious pies that Nellie has just baked puts you in a special class. A saint, Terraces brand, with no lights around the head. You are a man of great hunger, being stronger than we are. We have seen you, after long, lean days, weeping with joy at the sight of these pies and spoiling the pastry with your tears. Yet you give them away. Thank you, Ben.'

We told Ben's wife of how and why Eurona had been fasting for close on two days and not for a bet. Ben's wife took the news in her stride. She had long since used up her last stocks of amazement living with Ben and hearing his versions of the lectures and discussions we attended at the Library and Institute. She mothered Eurona in great style and laid her best table cloth in her honour. It was a cloth of brilliant colours. We could see the pleasure grow on Eurona's face. She had never seen such colours in the home of Morris except when Morris stuck his head up the chimney to be out of thought's way and brought a fall of soot down into the fire. We helped to set the pies out in very pretty pattern. We crowded around Eurona to help get her seated at the table. We were so eager at this she spent a few minutes thinking she was going to get through this meal sitting on our hands and she smiled shyly at us as if to say that she considered such a seat as being, while courteous, a bit too springy and mobile for her tastes. We gave her tea that had real milk and sugar in it. We had no butter to put on the bread but we asked Eurona to concentrate for all she was worth on the pies. We even put the gaslight on before it was properly dark to carry still further the impression that Eurona was being given a great celebration, the equivalent of a jubilee or a new throne in the lives of monarchs, no less intense for the fact that no one knew what was being celebrated. Some people collected outside in the back lane to smell the pies and pass on the time, stared long at this light, thinking, from seeing the gas lit so long before the sky had ceased to give forth light, that Ben had not been able to put it out from the night before. They hammered at Ben's back door and shouted over the wall that Ben should have this matter taken up with the gasworks. These people were very fond of Ben and did not want to see him out of pocket with his gas bills. Ben went outside and explained to these friends, that he meant the gas to be on and that this was a special occasion on which caution could go to the winds. He was prepared to spend as much as twopence over and above the normal and burn gas recklessly until such time as a platoon of gas men should come up the hill and order him to turn down his taps lest they should be driven to hire more miners to get the extra coal they would need to keep pace with the daring folly of one who put on the gas while the sun was still giving enough light to help you get around chairs and relatives without tripping on your face. When Ben came back in from this talk in the lane we could see he was grateful for the interest taken by these neighbours on his behalf. Grateful, he said, to them all except for the three voters who had been hammering on the door. They had come under the cloak of the others' kindness, not to warn him about the gas but for the door. That was their method. They would look out for any moment of public excitement, nip in and give a few hard blows at the door on which they had their eye. Having loosened the hinges, they could come around at a later and quieter hour and remove the door. They would then sell the door cheaply to a contractor, come home and write an ode on Natural Selection, they being the selected and the doorless one the natural. They had already done so well in their part of the Terrace people had lost their bearings on the old issue of in or out, having nothing to open or close. They had to borrow a door from some lucky neighbour who took no chances and served as his own hinge, use it intensely for an hour or so, before they regained something of their normal calm and sense of direction.

'Those boys plan to get on,' said Ben. 'They are probably children of Shadrach Sims, conceived during his period at the elementary school and ripened in vice during the early years of the Slump. They are starting with doors but there's no glory in doors. One of these days when a strong wind blows we'll hear moments of heavy knocking on the roof. Will that be the wind? No, it won't. It'll be these door-boys, new style, looking for that part of a house that does the same job for a house as hinges do for a door. Then it'll only be a case of choosing the night before we'll wake up in the morning on the ground with nothing above us but air and in our ears the laughter of these schemers putting our house down in the next valley, selling it for a song and coming back here to ask us to do part of the singing now that we have no housework to worry us. Shadrach would love them. So, if I understood those lectures down at the Library and Institute, would that boy Darwin.'

We grouped ourselves around the table again and encouraged Eurona to get on with her eating, to enjoy herself. We did not believe from the look of her that she understood what all the fuss was about but she grasped that people were trying to be kind to her. That in itself was a whole set of Northern Lights to Eurona. She smiled at us now and then as she made her way through the pies. My friend Ben stood at her shoulder and took a great interest in the way she was eating and staring at the pies as they vanished with a gleam in his eye as if they were part of his own person and Eurona his favourite cannibal. After every mouthful he asked her what she thought of the flavour.

'There are many ways of getting rid of flavour,' said Walter. 'But short of burning or burying the thing it's in, the best way is to be thrusting your ears into the mouth of the eater and inquiring about it every whipstitch.'

Ben moved back. The rest of us sat around trying in our various ways to look festive. We made a poor job of it because we had long since lost most of our skill in that line of conduct. We kept our conversation away from such topics as Rollo, the Assistance Board, the foxhunter and even the foxes, which were neutral in this matter of going away to work. We did not even make any general statements on the political situation which at that time like all other times would have benefited from a general statement by such types as ourselves who were pinned beneath the situation hardly able to breathe. We did not want to depress or baffle Eurona with deep or heavy themes until she had got over part of the blow she had received from meddling with love and Rollo. We dug up all the old jokes we could remember. We had to go around our minds with strong lanterns to find the places where we had to start digging. The jokes we dragged out may have been good in the days before the decline of the Terraces and the formalising of wit but either they had gone limp since or we had forgotten some of the points. Our approach was too thoughtful and our pace too leisurely to make indecency appear anything but indecent. We raised no smile on the face of Eurona and by her expression we judged that she must have been comparing the limp flat specimens of jokes we were telling with the shining up-to-date samples of dirt she had heard from Rollo during her short friendship with him. Ben was leaning against the sink in the further corner of the kitchen silent and absorbed in this new problem of light entertainment. Then he began laughing, showing that there was no longer any problem. His wife rushed to where he stood, thinking that Ben with his simple reliance on strength was now going to amuse Eurona with some practical and homely jape like tearing the sink off its hinges and juggling with it. She was still pressing hard against the wall plugs when Ben began his anecdote. He spoke it right out in a loud voice. It was a very bold joke stressing the animal side of man so baldly it made you wonder whether that tail bone in the back was really as short in your neighbour as in yourself. Ben kept laughing. He enjoyed every fume of it but he forgot that Eurona was not a sophisticated crone and that the joke needed to be cut down a yard and rehemmed with disinfectant thread before it could be put forward in the company of the young and unwitting. His wife had been drawing away from Ben during the telling of this whole tale. She looked at him with disgust. Then she told us slowly that if she had known that Ben had had this side to his character she would have turned him around more thoroughly in the

104

early stages. She waited for Ben to finish. The climax of the story was astonishing. She watched Ben as if he were sinking into a bog.

'With stuff like that lying about in your mind,' she said, 'the place for you, Ben, is not leaning against the sink but in it, even if it means badgering the landlord for a bigger sink.'

Then, having made this gesture to her Nonconformist forefathers and being a merrier person even than Ben, she laughed the loudest of us all.

*****

Later that evening we went along to the house of Rollo Watts to pass on to him the message we had received from Shadrach. Rollo was not at home. His parents came to the door and peeped out at us in a timid way, giving brief answers and making from moment to moment as if they were going to slam the door, call the police or start firing. This was because the parents of Rollo had never expected to see us or anyone like us standing at their door. They had always thought us strange, not so much because we had ideas that were different from their own. They did little in that field themselves. The fact that we had any ideas at all and allowed our eyes to darken with concern or trouble at what went on around us was enough for them. They looked at us around the edge of the door as if we had come with a brand for their burning or a placard around our necks announcing what bits of their furniture we had now decided to steal.

When we smiled at them and stated our business their manner changed. They opened the door wide and let us stand on the doorstep itself, our feet making a clumsy rustle on the gritty scouring. Rollo's mother went and fetched us some Welsh cakes and a glass apiece of nettle beer which, although it had a sourly herbal and cleansing taste, was refreshing. Mr Watts explained to us that Rollo had gone to the pictures with Clarisse, the young widow.

'A lovely couple,' he said. 'And a fine cinema that they've gone to, Mr Sims' Pontine Palace. Some very fine plush to be found there, I can tell you.'

'A wonderful couple,' added Mrs Watts as she handed around the cakes. 'They make a picture, Rollo and Clarisse. Not many couples like Rollo and Clarisse to be seen in these Terraces. If Frank, that's Mr Watts, gets a job in the new arsenal they're thinking of putting up and he's just the man for them after his four years in the last war, a shooter you know, we are going to help our Rollo buy Clarisse a fox fur.'

'I once saw a fox with one of those furs on but it didn't have the shape to set it off.'

'Splendid furs, those,' said Mr Watts. 'Splendid.'

'She'll look lovely, that Clarisse,' said Arthur, taking his key from Mr Watts but looking a bit stupefied by it as if still wondering what had brought us sticking our heads into this trap of talk about furs and couples and loveliness.

'When Rollo gets in with Shadrach Sims,' said Ben, 'he can also have a wolf skin for himself. Very warm for his work on the buses.'

Mr Watts looked keenly at Ben, as if still doubtful about our credentials.

106

'Yes,' he said tentatively. 'A big man, Shadrach Sims. Big enough to buy up these Terraces.'

'Big enough, but not daft enough,' said Walter.

'Shadrach Sims, daft?' asked Mr Watts, alarmed.

'No, no. Not daft. He wouldn't waste his money on these Terraces. They haven't got a future.'

'I wouldn't say that.'

'You wouldn't say it, Mr Watts, because you'd think it over too carefully. That makes you the man you are. But we four are the most reckless pack of sods you'll ever see. We say the first thing that comes into our heads.'

'Bad thing, that.'

'Too true, it is.'

'Stands in a man's light very often, this blurting.'

'We owe most of our misery to blurting. Wish we'd had your sense years ago, Mr Watts. But some men take time to learn. But we've learned now. We are not like we were. After hearing the views of Shadrach Sims we have come to see that there's a lot to be said for the wealthy. So from now we're going to keep what we think to ourselves even if the grievances come to us of their own accord and offer to pay us for an opinion. From now on we're going to be like the shops of this area, shut up for the most part.'

'A wise decision. There'll be a war soon.' Mr Watts said that in a slow, grave voice and paused, as if waiting to see us look amazed. When he found we took the forecast in our stride he went on: 'Work will be coming our way again. But not for everybody. Oh no. The people on top won't forget the people on the bottom who've shown during these slack years that they have no confidence in the country.'

107

'Of course they won't. They're not fools. But we'll soon make them forget we ever said anything out of place or on the sad side. We'll even cut our nods down by half. We'll have so much confidence in the country you'll see the country bucking up and grinning with pleasure under your very eyes.'

'You ought to hear our Rollo on that very point. He's wonderful.'

'I bet he is. We're looking forward to hearing him. So's Mr Sims. Rollo won't be needing the bus company once he gets in well with Mr Sims.'

'We always saw a golden future for Rollo.'

'You have a fine son, Mr Watts.'

So there we stood for thirty minutes on the doorstep of the Watts family. We ate our cakes and thumbed away crowds of kids who came near thinking that this eating and drinking in the open could only be the beginning of some broader celebration like a street party to celebrate the passing of the landlord and finding that the same tenants were still in the street. Some of these children looked so yearning we gave them a sip or two of the nettle beer. That cured them. They went.

While we waited we decided to let Mr and Mrs Watts have the floor. It was their doorstep and it was very hard to find anything to say to this Watts that did not cause him to rub vinegar on his brow to clear his brain or crinkle up his miniature forehead and wonder whether the remark you had just made was on the right side of the law. Here again we were made solemn by an awareness of the fact that hope and thought seemed to be poised in a bitter and destructive rivalry.

Mrs Watts had been for many years in domestic work with one of the country's premier landowning families. This family, by a smooth alliance of pen and sword, had helped itself to a record tract of hills and valleys. If the earth were iron filings and these people magnets they would have done no better. From her stay with this favoured group Mrs Watts had contracted a philosophy of chronic servility which had filled her mental joints with barrowloads of agonising crystals. The slightest thought of discontent and her ears turned black and dipped an inch for shame. We could see her mind, after a lot of peering, crawling with relish towards any object that seemed likely to respond to the act of worship. Up against Mrs Watts the average mat had a swaggering air of erect independence. She told us of the gay times her young mistresses, the three daughters of the family, had had in the revels held at the mansion in the days before the bill for enlarged social services came in in a black tide and dowsed the lights around the great hall one by one. They were the days of the hunt in all its glory, brilliant hospitality lavished at the hunt balls. Ben nodded a lot at this point as if this were the one feature of the whole narrative that he clearly understood. He bent his head forward as Mrs Watts went on in breathless glee to tell us more of the hunt balls. She told us of the floods of light, the streams of silk and wine, all come together at the call of magic and romance for a few glowing nights each year to make landowning seem worth while and to compensate these weary hunters and dancers for the stooped gait and dejection of mind they sustained in the cause of keeping their fields wholesome – Ben nodded understandingly again – and their tenants at ease and secure. Yes, they were the days of beauty and revel, the days of the great balls.

'No,' said Ben, 'we don't get the feeding we used to.'

'They went on till three in the morning, the little misses, and still laughing like little fairies, didn't they, Frank?'

'Like little fairies,' said Frank, looking at that moment quite rapt and, in his bluish, diaphanous fragility, rather like a small elf himself.

'What were you then, Frank?' asked Ben who seemed to have entered with whole soul into this discussion of revels and balls.

'I once had the honour,' said Mr Watts, 'to serve for a short time as junior footman at the great house.' He spoke here in a voice of great depth and dignity, pouring a spoonful of treacle over every word.

'Footman?' said Ben. 'What were you doing with your foot, Frank?'

'I was attendant to the master.'

'With buttons right up to the neck,' said Mrs Watts.

'Why, these two poor bastards were no better than serfs,' said Ben.

Mr and Mrs Watts bridled slowly.

'Ben was talking to those two kids over there,' said Walter, pointing to a pair of lads a few yards away who were queueing up for a sip and a bite.

'Oh.'

Then we had some more memories. Mrs Watts recalled the names and shapes and pedigrees of the ponies the little misses had ridden. She described the rousing canters they had, shouting halloo, hello, bravo and God knows what other words of a like fatuous cut at the tenants who stood about baring their heads, opening the gates at the same time as their mouths to put on a kind of double gape, bowing low and otherwise, in company with Mr and Mrs Watts, giving up the mental ghost with such brutal haste we could imagine the ghost pausing with anguish on its face in some far, penultimate suburb of the skull on its way out and wondering what it had done to deserve all this. We could imagine too the little misses putting the saddle on Mrs Watts and giving the ponies a rest whenever they came to some specially steep climb like the sheer face of a quarry.

'But the Days,' said Mrs Watts. 'The Days were the great hunt balls.'

'Tell me,' said Arthur who had been listening puzzled to the tale of these feudal antics. 'What were these balls? What purpose did they serve? Who was being hunted? Was it the people who had fallen behind with the rent? Were they given any start and who did the hunting?'

Mr and Mrs Watts looked at him blankly. Even Ben looked at Arthur as if he were letting down some fine old tradition.

'These balls,' said Walter, 'were events similar to our Sunday School treats but with fewer benches, no pictures from the Bible on the walls, more jelly and altogether less to do with God.'

'I have always striven,' said Mrs Watts, raising her hand and letting her voice tremble as if she were making some unique, momentous admission of an inner faith, 'to make

111

our own Rollo just such a gentleman as the master of the old hall.'

'Bring the iron lung,' said Ben to me in a mutter. 'These people are in a worse state than Morris.'

Then Mr Watts passed on some more time with tales of boxing. That was his fancy. He had clearly read every word about this sport that had appeared in the Sunday papers for the past thirty years. If these legions of boxers about whom he spoke with such detail had been his brothers he could not have been more fluent. We could imagine him crouched in the outside water closet of a long Sunday morning, wrapped up in the latest memoirs of the oldest referees, making careful notes on the whitewashed wall and pushing back bits off the roof with his Boy Scout's pole every time he wanted to relieve eye strain.

'I've done a bit at the old game myself,' he said, winking and grinning and twitching his body about in a way we have noted to be common among timid people who are screwing themselves up to a discussion of the thing they prize most highly in their essential selves. He began dodging about in front of us, weaving cleverly with his body, making quick passes with his hands, increasing his speed with every second and working his way up to be a blur. During the few seconds when he appeared to come to rest, he raised the back of his right hand to his nose and blew on it with a passion that made us feel he was now fighting to the last breath in his body and this was it.

'The blood,' he said, explaining this blowing. 'The other bloke has just landed me a hard one on the nose and I'm keeping the channel free.' He blew again and we stepped back to give the other bloke all the room he needed to do even more damage to Mr Watts. Mrs Watts watched him with a look on her face of beaming and rotund satisfaction. She winked at us as if to say that we were now indeed watching something we had never bargained to see. We winked back as if to say that we certainly were. Watts brought his tactics to bear on each one of us in turn and treated us to about thirty seconds apiece. Even if he had not blinded you with science he would swiftly have made you weary of looking. He did all this without any word of comment further to what he had already said about his nose. He did not even break silence when some neighbour, thinking from his motions that he was beating off a pack of assailants, offered to close in from the rear. To end, he said he would show us ten punches, five of which would kill. We watched him go through this course in butchery and listened to his gasping, grinning, delighted talk of split kidneys, numbed jugulars and nerves that came away on your glove. We felt how glad we were to have lived in the Terraces for so long without before having come into active commerce with this little menace.

'And now,' he said, 'I will show you the very blow that Morgan Haynes of Howell Street used to send Nally Williams of Bendegedig Terrace fifteen feet into the air.'

For this he seemed to wind himself up like a watch, arranging his legs and arms in a series of knots that it seemed idle to follow. Then he unleashed, as if set off with the red end of a poker. He seemed to whirr. He went nearly as far up as Nally Williams. For all we knew, Haynes may well have escorted Williams on the trip. It was a nice change to have Watts above us for a spell. From what little we could see of his face he was as surprised to be as far from the earth as that as we were. When he came back to the ground it was with a bang that shook him to the last fibre.

'They called me The Tiger,' he said, as soon as he had his limbs running once more in the same direction. 'Can you imagine that?' The fall had obviously given the shy small fancy of this man an impulse of adventure. We decided to stroke his illusion until it purred. 'Yes,' we said. And so we could. With prompting we can imagine anything.

'I was small and not too strong. But there were old hands at the game who said they had never seen the like of my footwork. At the end, it got so good it was a hindrance. I baffled myself even. I couldn't stop still at all and I knew as little as the man facing me about where I'd turn up next.'

'For the first year of our marriage,' said Mrs Watts, 'he was a terror. The Tiger was a Terror.' The words delighted her. 'He had to have one leg strapped to the rail of the bed and even then I had to get out off and on to keep the bed in the room. One man told me Frank's leg had the strength of two horses. He worked that bed like a motor.'

'Oh I was a marvel,' said Watts.

I wondered if that was what he meant by being a footman.

'I have always striven,' said Mr Watts, with the same raised hand and shaking voice as we had seen in Mrs Watts 'to bring up my son Rollo in the best traditions of British self defence. Rollo is a true son of Queensberry.'

'You mean...' started Ben, then stopped, afraid of risking yet another insult to Mr Watts that evening.

114

We surveyed Mr and Mrs Watts with a new under-standing. Domestic labour, a glad acceptance of masters, Sunday papers, the steady renunciation of a present that seemed grey against a golden past, had made a pair of masterpieces of these two, small but in every detail of line and form, perfect.

Rollo and Clarisse came around the corner into the street where we were waiting. His hair had a wavy brilliance that seemed to sound in the air like one of those harps they used to hang in trees. We were again reminded that this young man's head had taken on most of the lustre that had been lost by the coal trade when the Navy went over to oil. He wore his golfing trousers. Even from where we stood we could feel the passion come beating from these two like the air from a tapped furnace. Clarisse was a dark, heavy-faced, broad-hipped woman, an ever open booth for the roaring thoughtless heat into which the whole being of Rollo had been transformed. His face was near to hers and glowing like a gas fire. He was clutching her even as he walked. We thought with a furtive irony of how little chance Eurona would have had even with a few gold mesh vests thrown in by the Board to help on the yellow fabric and the Fixo, of spiking the guns of this Clarisse's skilled, broad-calibre desires. From behind us Mr and Mrs Watts were uttering cries of glee at the mere sight of Rollo. These cries affected me badly, like the rub of paper on wood. I found myself having the thought that it would be nicer if people would have children without bothering to plague and unbalance them by passing on to these children their own opinions of them to become an active and terribly unchanging base for any future thoughts these children might have about themselves. Parents should be strictly neutral until the child has reached middle age. As Rollo came in sight of his parents his face dropped to a lower gear of incandescence and assumed a noble quietude. They, it was obvious, had built this youth into the position of that sun god Ra, pronounced by them, Ro, with ice cream all around. And Rollo, having given the thing all the thought he could muster without tearing his ears off to make more room, could not see in what particular they could possibly be wrong.

He frowned as he saw us. We were in no way the sort of products he wanted to see outside his door except attached by stout cord to the lintel with our feet away from the ground and not dirtying the well scoured sill. He linked us with the sordid democratic notions such as wanting pay for work which, in Rollo's view, had degraded the Terraces into a privy of mud and mediocrity. Our hair was not wavy or brilliant. It was either not there or flat. Our trousers were sub-normal, not knickered but still finding it difficult to reach the top of our boots without asking us to bend our legs. My friend Walter explained to him that we had come as the envoys of Shadrach Sims who was interested in Rollo and wished to have talk with him and that we, too, were men, long immersed in degradation and error, but now convinced that youth, together with those shiny novelties of thought and toilet that Rollo sponsored, must have their day if the Terraces, grown corrupt with sloth and delusion, were not to die. Rollo's face did not relax as he listened to what Walter had to say. He was feeling the gentle rub of destiny against his being, hoping it was not a dog, and trying hard not to look selfconscious and unrubbed. He surveyed us with what he would have called chilly hauteur. It was obvious that he had long been practising this look before mirrors and in house windows. The parts of his face moved into position like troops into a battle line. He was prepared to accept us as envoys or as incense bearers but we were to keep our distance. We would need, to his mind, a lot of scrubbing and sprinkling before the old smell of rebellion grew faint enough on our bodies for his liking.

'I have work to do,' said Rollo. 'I must prepare a statement of my views for Mr Sims. With a man like Mr Sims one will need method.'

Clarisse was delighted. This revelation about Shadrach wishing to anoint Rollo with his favour must have come as the final sweet on a long evening of intense and toothsome canoodling in the darker reaches of the Pontine Palace and she danced around Rollo in a way that, for such a heavily built girl, was deft and nimble.

Rollo nodded gravely at her to make her pause in her dancing.

'But it's wonderful,' she said. 'They always told me that our ideas would never win a hearing in these Terraces. And soon you will be heard. Mr Sims is too big a man not to appreciate your dynamic message of the Regenerate Will, too wise a man not to wish to see you slap it hard across the unlit skulls of these moaning slummies.'

We did a little background moaning and turned up the wick for Rollo to get busy with the match while she resumed her excited dancing. Another nod from Rollo, still grave with the sense of mission, bade her cease, as if telling her that when there is a tide in the affairs of toads that does not justify even the bull frog's firstline passion in behaving like a tadpole on the turn. He walked inside without giving us a further glance. His parents followed him closely as if drawn by a painful magnetism.

'God above,' said Ben, 'I'd like to go in there and show Mr Watts, with Rollo as my raw material, the blow that sent Meirion Saunders of Fountain Row seventeen feet into the air.'

'Ne'er cast a clout,' said Arthur, 'till maypole be out.'

*****

Morris went half mad when he found that we four were now to become part of Shadrach Sims' bill sticking and advertising retinue. He would not have been more numbed with surprise if we had gone on to him, taller, darker and sweeter than usual and explained that we had just come back from a course of training as date trees. It would be hard to say what exactly Morris thought of Shadrach Sims for the mind of this man was a deep shadowed glade where thoughts were seen dimly like animals that go down to drink but pause in dread of the hunter who will always be waiting for them at the brink of the pool. Take the opinions of Mr and Mrs Watts on the subject of Rollo, beat up in a pail of fluid gold and you had Morris' notion of Shadrach. Morris might have spoken casually to you of God but this close contact with a man who owned a chain of grocery shops would have left him with the silence that follows the great wind of some emotion that leaves no stone in the scrubby patch of our being untouched, unturned. As we watched Morris when we told him of our preferment, we could hear the wind begin to blow within him and the stones begin to stir and heave. He was almost doing cartwheels with the shock when we told him that on the very next morning we would be walking down the Terraces to do paid work again and when we told him what the wage would be gave out a sound that was like a drowned laugh floating to the surface of a groan and ran to the nearest soft grassy patch where he slumped down in a trance of wonder. When he returned he pointed at us with his forefinger, saying nothing, his mouth wide open and gasping as if we had kicked him in the stomach. Together with the natural look of grief and oppression in his eye this caused several passers-by of an earnest and interfering kind to come on to us and say that we should be ashamed of ourselves to be hitting the stomach of a man like Morris whose stomach was so small it needed a black heart to hit it and a pretty sharp eye to find it at all. It got on Arthur's nerves to have Morris trailing us like that and attracting the attention of all people who were out to prevent cruelty of this sort and that. We told him to go home and read something hopeful and strengthening. But he was in a state of galloping excitement. He had not been as near Olympus since that great day in the last war when the Angel of Mons had nodded to him and told him that all would be well, showing how wrong angels can be when they take sides in a war. He seemed even to have forgotten the trouble that would come upon Eurona when the Government and the foxhunter took some time off from the chase and began to compare notes and evil intentions.

The manager of Shadrach's main store in the bottom Terrace gave us the bills and paste and brush. When Morris saw us with all this equipment he knew finally that this whole development was real and not a sardonic mirage pressed by anguish from his brain. Even had he found us to be lying he would have thanked us gravely for the privilege of sharing in a rich, consoling fancy. He walked behind Ben staring hard at the paste which was the same colour as his brain, his past, his skin, his future and his ancient shapeless hanging suit. He even dipped his finger furtively and quickly into the stuff, sucked it and looked delighted.

'For Christ's sake, Morris,' said Ben who was already ill enough at ease forming one of this odd little parade led by Walter who was carrying the brush and looked as intent and expert as if he were going to repaint the roof of that chapel in Rome. 'Go home and nibble away at your problems in private. We'll bring the tin and what's left of the paste to your house tonight and you can eat your fill in comfort. But be careful to leave some around your mouth and if you can carve some slogans on your chest and stomach boosting up Shadrach and his provisions we'll stick you up on the boards with the other bills tomorrow.'

'Carve?' asked Morris seriously, believing Ben and nearly delirious at the thought of being part of this adventure, even a part on the wrong end of the brush.

We set out on our route. Shadrach had left us free to cover the beat in our own way. I had an armful of leaflets in thick black type bearing messages that were easy to unravel, like 'Save large sums, with Sims'. 'Who WAS first? Sims. Who IS first? Sims', or, more intimate, 'Who'll build your children healthy limbs? Sims', 'Who'll stand by you through good and bad? Shad!' 'Whose cheese is smooth as our well-loved hymns? Sims'. Morris received a strong emotion from these sentences. I could see him standing still to get the full flavour and meaning, as if they were healing breezes blowing in upon his feeble body from the sea. Now and then he would stop a child, fix it with a stare or a mild clip and reel off the whole programme of mottoes and couplets he had learned from the handbills. He would stand by my side as I explained to the dozier voters who came straight to the door from bed and thought from my sincere praise of Sims that I must be Sims, what I was there for. He would nod fiercely as I spelled out the simpler axioms for these slow moving types and told them that Shad would stick by them through good and bad, that Sims would build their children healthy limbs. Morris' mouth would move solemnly over the same words as mine, never ceasing to nod and crane his body against mine like a grey convulsive shadow. The drowsy ones, paying more attention to the antics of Morris than to my propaganda, would conclude that since yesterday, when things had indeed been looking as if they may be on the turn, the world had gone mad as well as poor and back they went to bed where, given reasonable good will on the part of the bed's legs, it was at least safe.

When we were sticking one of the larger bills to a wall or a hoarding, Morris stood back looking at us with a knowing pride as if he had been keeping us back as an unanswerable shot in the proletarian locker and as if any hands but ours on Shadrach's brush would have meant disaster for the grocery trade. Whether anyone were passing or not we could hear him say as he pointed to us: 'Friends of mine. Known them for years. Told them to keep fresh for this day. Their chance has come. Enough paste there to plaster the bloody Terraces from top to tail with stuff about Sims. Through good and bad, Shad. Fine little poem that. And my chance will come too. When you see those boys over there moving about sticking things up we're on the move. Just watch me. It'll come.'

People whom he stopped and talked to, seeing perhaps no link between Morris and their own brand of reality, dismissed him as a buffoon whose line was a morbid and grotesque humour of which one could quickly have too much. We were fixing a bill on the side of a bridge when Shadrach Sims came up to see how we were getting along. He was on foot and splendidly turned out in a new blue suit. We were having difficulty in getting the bill straight for we had spent many years in a medium of experience where crookedness and its opposite were concepts that had become generalised and tenuous. Frankly it did not seem to matter half a damn to us whether all this literature about Sims was straight or on the slope. There were many voters in the Terraces who were on a kind of slope themselves, their minds and bodies poised on mouldered and softened foundations, who would be, if anything, grateful for a bend in the print. Many others there were so slow to read and slower still to buy from Sims or anyone else, a poster put on upside down would have been just their fancy.

Morris did not know Shadrach by sight and took him to be someone, a chance stroller, interested as anyone in his senses was bound to be in the very fine job we were doing with the bills. He came across the road to tell Shadrach what good friends of his we were and what a golden day this was in the lives of us, paste, Sims, the Terraces and himself. The sight of him, suddenly and without any warning, beheld, with his incredible suit and his air of dumb and strangely wrought remoteness, his smile trying to break through his melancholy greyness like sun through mist, scared the wits out of Shadrach.

'No, no!' he shouted, jumping from the approaching Morris as if he were being offered a pint of poison.

'All right,' said Walter, thinking that Shadrach was complaining about the brave angle at which he had laid on the poster.

'No, no!' shouted Shadrach again as Morris circled for an opening and doubled the brilliance of his smile which only made matters worse. Morris even tugged at his waistcoat to make it sit more neatly and we could hear the last two or three stitches of the shoulder seams go their way home causing Morris to lift both his arms swiftly to his shoulder blades to keep the waistcoat somewhere about him. This new stance did not help him with Shadrach.

'All right,' said Walter. 'Jack it up a bit on your side, Ben. Mr Sims is fussier about these things than we are. Don't you worry, Mr Sims, we'll get right into the strategy of this pasting shortly. We're a lot better now than we were when we started two hours ago. The first two we stuck were on the floor because that's the only place where we've been

123

doing any steady looking for a long time past. Our neck muscles have been limp and no good for forward gazing since the day when King Arthur hit us over the head with the grail and told us how he had been getting fees from ten directors' boards for keeping us boys on tenterhooks with dreams of seeing him walk back one day from Avalon. It would never have dawned on us to seek news about groceries on high, outlandish places like walls.'

Morris could not follow exactly what Walter was saying but he guessed from the shape of Walter's eyes that it was probably something which could from some angles be treated as a jest. He put his head back and gave out a cackle that would have sent a chicken keeper racing for the cot. Shadrach stepped behind Ben and looked out at Morris impressed but unbelieving. Morris was pleased at having caught Shadrach's attention. He was going to repeat the cackle to make quite sure when Walter flagged him, for pity's sake, to stop.

'I wasn't talking about the way you have of shoving those bills up at all angles,' said Mr Sims. 'As a matter of fact I like the way you do it. By the time the people have spent a month rubbing in all the liniment they'll need to forget the crick in the neck they'll get from trying to read these bills without having one leg shorter than the other, they'll never forget it was Sims' groceries they read about when they finally got the message into focus from between their legs. No, it was this bloke I was shouting at, this bleached man who just made that noise. He's not genuine. I've made up my mind about that. He's no more genuine than a wig.'

124

'He's genuine all right,' said Walter. 'He's a man without any shadow of doubt, is Morris. Count his limbs. They add up to the right number. Watch his eyes move when they are not just standing still wondering what's to do. He's a man all right. He gets insurance from the Government. You won't find the Government giving these benefits to animals. They're so strict, you wouldn't believe.'

'I mean the way he looks. I know he's a man. He's somewhere near the shape. But his clothes, his boots, that look on his face. Nobody could look like that without making a special job of it, without being paid. He's an actor. He's up to something. He's hired to do this by the anarchists and the levellers in an attempt to horrify the Government and the well-to-do.'

'No, honest,' answered Walter. 'This Morris is a known and well loved man in the Terraces. He's been on the Insurance for a long time. They launched the scheme with him. They broke a stamp over his head and he whistled like a steamer when he signed his name for the first time in the register to prove he was alive and had at least one hand. But there's nothing about the look of this man that's sensational. There are Terraces where Morris would quickly become a snob as people pestered him for the right to wait crouched at his knee caps to catch his waistcoat if it drops and he keeps standing or to get into it if he drops and it keeps standing. If he is an actor, the only part he could play is life on the crumble. He just got bleached by worry and weariness of being the same old human colour all the time. And as for trying to horrify the well-to-do and the Government Mr Sims, we have tried to do that too. It

125

can't be done. They're up to our every trick. They've even learned how to pull us right through when we try to blow at them into the key holes. So we gave up. We just stand still now and let them horrify us.'

'Queer blokes, you,' said Shadrach. 'You really seem to have minds that work, but darkly and into living instead of along it. You should give away a match with every sentence so that people who still believe in summer can strike up and follow the drift of what you say. So he always looks like that, does he?' Shadrach sat down on a wooden seat provided as a halting place on the sharply climbing road by the Council. He lit a cigarette and gestured to Morris to walk about in front of him so that all the points could be taken in. Morris stiffened with a sense of responsibility but could not bring himself to move until we started to shove at his back and shout words of friendship and encouragement at him. Then he began to parade back and fore in front of the reflective Shadrach like a grenadier, his torn waistcoat making rapidly for the ground as his body, contracted with this new and fierce dignity, failed to give it the subtle support of outthrust bones and joints.

'If he stamps any harder,' said Ben, 'we'll have to catch his head every time it bounces.'

'He's putting the last ounce of his strength into this marching,' said Walter. 'This is as good a bit of marching over a short distance as I've ever seen. If nothing comes of this it'll snap Morris like a twig and he'll do the rest of his travelling on a handcart.'

Shadrach studied Morris hard. He was obviously moved to a headful of thought by this incident. He motioned

Morris to a halt and called the five of us to come and stand around his seat, looking grave. 'I see now,' he said. 'Upon you all is this terrible ravaging sadness. Within some there is the steel knot of pride or obstinacy or even sheer damned daftness that refuses to be flattened by the falling sky. But others,' he pointed at Morris, 'others exist for the pure reason and love of being crushed. They like counting the pieces that are left over, even put them in position for the cruncher and wait for the great day when they can introduce themselves to the family as a box of the finest powder, the family's first and only gift from the old man. It is these fibreless oafs whose lips are fixed and sucking at your hearts. It is they who have made the burial hymns our national balm for so long, if you want to see the Creative Will you have to go along to the toilet, knock on the door and tell it it can now come out for a short airing.'

'We ought to do something about it,' said Walter.

'We will.'

'We knew you'd say that, Mr Sims. Believe it or not this Morris was full of the Will and as keen as anybody to get on and make something of himself until he got a kitchenful of daughters and his suit ran down.'

Shadrach's eyes lit up at the sound of the word daughters as if the thought of woman induced in him an easy reflex. We noted this with interest for it would have taken the sight of a dozen girls like Salome being efficient, and fireworks let into the back of the head to make our eyes light up at the mention of this topic. But the light died soon away from Shadrach's eyes. His mind was clearly at an angle from which maidens slipped away.

127

'How would you like a new suit?' he asked Morris.

Morris kept staring at Shadrach without reaction. The question loaded with all the daring strangeness of a pervert's dream, aimed at the shy and distant consciousness of Morris fell away far short of the mark.

'Ask him,' said Shadrach, thinking that all communications with Morris might need some touch of explanatory gesture or dialect.

'Mr Sims is wanting to give you a new suit, Morris,' translated Walter. 'How would you like that? A suit. A full, new suit.'

The next thing we heard was a slither of rubble beneath the feet of Morris and a gasp from Arthur as he found himself holding the senseless Morris.

'It was too abrupt,' said Walter. 'You should have broken it to him in smoke signals first. We have known men who died from hearing things much less astonishing than that.'

Ben held the cool side of the paste pot against Morris' brow. He recovered with only the slightest coaxing from us. Shadrach wrote him a slip in voucher form, gave him the name of the store where we had bought those clothes for Eurona and told Morris to hand it to the manager. Morris looked weakly from one face to the next, wishing to be reassured, told that this whole scene, tasselled with Arabia's richest silks, was no mere chill on the kidneys giving him the willies and the visions. We nodded and smiled at him as hard as we could to show him that the world, for motives cheerful or sinister but as yet unknown, was really doing these things. He turned on Shadrach, sick with gratitude. Shadrach stepped once more away. Morris, determined to make public some fragment of the writhing, unskilled ecstasy within him, stood still and erect and let off another of those cackles. There was no movement in him that we could see to show from what part of his body he produced this racket. Even his glottis, normally protrusive and waving about like a third arm, hung in a sad, neutral suspension in the middle of his neck. Just this chime of mad, momentary concordance from this inharmonious shadow of a man. Then he bolted off without a word.

'The sight of that man tidied up will surely clear a part of the jungle for a settlement of new dignity and ambition,' said Shadrach. 'He should be exhibited in every British town. Before and after. Did you notice whether he had parts of his jacket tied on to his hair to hold it up?'

'I'm not sure but Morris will make any little changes you fancy.'

'Yes, exhibited. Do the world of good. The shock of seeing him in an outfit that allows the sleeves of his coat to be distinguished from the legs of his trousers may give many of you a new faith.'

'It will,' said Walter. 'Even as we stand here now we can feel the miracle of Morris working on us like a fertility rite.'

Shadrach looked up at the sky, pulled in at his cigarette until his eyes became smoky and gave his head a sudden shake. He went off without a further sound, almost as quickly as Morris but with less reason. For the first time seeing the man as a man and not as a blotch of money and influence, we felt something strange and distracted in him, a discord as chilling as came forth from the long night of Morris.

129

'Walter,' said Ben taking the seat on the Council bench that Shadrach had left. 'There are many things about you that I've never understood. To those things, boyo, I now add this problem: why the hell should you want to see Shadrach making a gift of all this splendour to Morris. Haven't you already had as much trouble with the clothing question in the Morris family as we as a body have had with such issues as full employment, equality, hell and rent. Didn't that Eurona teach you a lesson or have we reached some new wisdom whose heart is to laugh at lessons. Didn't it show that if we people look dead, are thought of as dead, that we should at least have the pleasure of acting dead and not give a damn whether our neighbours are naked or clothed. Or are you trying to doll this Morris up to such toffee apple standard that will cause Rollo to grow to love him too and then have Rollo put away in gaol for the unchristian quality of his lusts, Morris being no woman. If so, I can't see it coming off unless you fit up Morris with a suit of double-breasted magnets and Rollo in a shirt of iron mail.'

'Have a little patience, Ben,' said Walter. 'Given a leaky economic order, these Terraces, human feelings coming down in a heavy rain, a group of people not dressed for the wet, whose wits are on the rot and whose wills twitch to the strange music of mountains and privation, you would be surprised what interesting sketches can be arranged.'

'Tell me when each sketch ends,' said Ben, 'and I will laugh and clap.'

We resumed our work. In mid-afternoon we heard our names called. It was a far faint voice and we could not see the caller. At first we felt this voice might be part of a delirium brought by the task of holding the trumpet through which Shadrach Sims was blowing to awaken the Terraces to a new sense of their own hunger. The last stage in this curious process of alienation would be a pilgrimage unpaid and in our own time, converted now to the culture of self-esteem that drives our trading adventurers forward on their half pint odyssey, from street to street telling the occupants that we wished, with all the sincerity in this world, to ask them who would fill their cups of economic and social well being to the brim. Sims. Whose jams would make the old folks glad? Shad. And for the higher-toned residential areas of the valley, whose bread will make you eat in bed? Shad. And we would believe all this, eager to take refuge in any assertion that would distract us from the thought of our own withering forlornness. Then around a corner came a purplish, glowing patch moving towards us like a comet. We were prepared to believe that this might well be a small typhoon presented by the authorities in glorious technicolour to go sucking up the Terraces one by one, picking the voters up and turning them inside out and proving to us that man's ineptitude which had been our particular vulture to date was still slower on the peck and gentler on the pelt than nature in her bloodier pranks.

'Am I seeing colours never before seen among these hills?' asked Arthur. 'Or am I having a spell put on my stomach by this paste?'

'Good God,' I said, dropping thousands of Sims' handbills. 'It's Morris.'

Morris it was. He had run hard and far. He was not so much breathless as pumped clean out and waiting for the

day when he could repay life the forty gasps he had
overdrawn. We approached him from different angles,
cautiously, allowing the fact and colour of this suit he had
on to break on us by inches, like light on the eyes of one
learning to see again. It was that very suit, that mad
affirmation in mauve and red that had so caught his eye on
the day when we had gone around the shop with Eurona. It
was Morris' total, rebelling answer to all the monochrome
littleness of his days on earth. It was the sickening hallellu-
jah of one who has been mute and without the need for
exultation so long he does not know what tone to use to
please or hurt or still be mute. From the moment he had
received the written slip from Shadrach he had homed to
that suit as if beauty, on the eve of its final hounding from
our midst, had hidden all her secrets in its seams as a refuge
against the day when we would once more rise to the desire
for beauty and the courage to go forth to seek it. Not even
the shrewdest and most cunning of those who have no love
for beauty would have sought it there to work their hatred
on it. The suit was a shade big but once you had calmed
down to an acceptance of the colours, it was Morris' hat
that took hold of your eye and put its foot against the socket
to heave. It was a bowler, a bowler many sizes too big for
Morris. It must, without any need for tape measure or
question, have been the biggest bowler in the Terraces.
Morris' head, long whittled by a hail of events that were so
little serene or even intelligible, seemed to have shrunk. If
Morris' landlord had been a Samoan headhunter with the
proper apparatus of hot sand, illwill and scoop to do this job
of shrinking and pin Morris' head on his lapel to put the

fear of God into his other tenants, a better job could not have been done on Morris. His ears appeared to be closing in on him for they were large and made larger by the fact that when Morris was baffled beyond endurance, he had two of his children take one ear apiece and pull to make room within his skull even for the small simple thoughts that ached to have done with him as they tripped headlong in the narrow alleys of his prickly awareness. To fix the bowler at a point above his eyes he had stuffed several sheets of newspaper into it. This stuffing had been done in haste and clumsily. One strand with a legible headline about the birthrate came down over his brow as if to provide him with some quiet reading in the intervals of being admired and fainting from the strain of holding up on so slight a head a hat of such weight and size.

'How do I look?' he asked.

We were silent for a whole minute, dipping our souls in respect to the force that had laboured this entire antic to such a glossy finish. It was as if God on the seventh day had looked down and asked diffidently, 'Is it big enough, round enough, bad enough?'

'Morris,' said Arthur. 'You will be the sweetheart of the nether prolies, the idol of all who toil; a statue to you in pepsin and monkey nuts will be raised in the lobby of the Pontine Palace and eaten in your honour. You are a glory to us all, Morris, and the first genuine consolation yet to be offered to those boys whose nystagmus will keep you more or less invisible. You are a cough drop, friend.'

'It is middling useful,' said Morris, unbuttoning his coat to let himself swell with pride and bring the stripes an inch

133

or so nearer our eyes. He did something to the air. He seemed to shake and snake about in front of us.

'But that hat,' said Walter. 'You've pulled off a big job there, Morris. How do you explain it? Did it drop on you from somewhere?'

'It's been crouching on a roof for years waiting to get him,' said Ben. 'No bowler that knows its job could ever love Morris. Bowlers are much too black ever to forget a grudge, especially against a pale voter like Morris.'

'I got it from that dead bloke,' said Morris.

'You mean you got it away from somebody just before they boxed him? That was a daring stroke, boy. That suit's giving you new skill.'

'No no. This bloke I'm talking about has been dead for a good time.'

'Tell us who; the dead are many. We want to know which of the dead you chose when deciding to rob a grave of that article.'

'This hat belonged to Tudor Phelps. You remember Tudor, the good reciter, the man with the big head, the man who always said he agreed with death.'

'We do. We often agreed with Tudor. He had a big head, as you say. For that reason some of the boys here in the Terraces called Tudor The Bucket. But that wasn't fair for Tudor was full of thought.'

'He was and all,' said Morris, seeming to stretch his arm out to the full to stroke the side of his bowler. 'If death would speak it would have mentioned Tudor as one of its most devoted friends. You could see him thinking of it all the time. And he wasn't ever ill. That was the beauty of it.

134

He was a real amateur, Tudor. He was for death through thick and thin.'

'Who scorns death though no one helps? Phelps,' said Arthur mechanically.

'Who will brood in every mood? Tude,' seconded Ben.

'You're right,' went on Morris, 'Somebody once said they saw a cypress growing from the back of Tudor's neck but that must have been a shadow for who ever heard of trees growing in that quarter. He was always in funerals. Keeping his foot in, he called it. That's why he bought this splendid bowler. Always kept it shiny and in good trim. He always said I could borrow it any time I liked. Tudor always had a soft spot for me, said I reminded him of a real bit of the old beyond, me being on the frail and anaemic side. And it's coming very nicely to my size and shape too. I've only got to use two *Western Mail*s and the thick cover of the *Picture Post*. Last time I wore it I used a round of linoleum as well. But now it fits a treat.'

'You could have done with a second head,' said Walter, 'or a friend, who'd have stuck his own up and not minded being slap up against you. Yes, that's a fine thickness of paper you've got there, Morris. If that bowler was transparent you'd make a nice open air reading room for the boys who like their education standing up and find the Library and Institute too stuffy.'

We fell silent. Morris let his eyes wander up and down his suit. Then a slight shudder shot its bolt through his body. He looked straight at us, putting his hand abruptly over his mouth to stop the twitching of his lips. He would have found it easy to weep and we would have known from this gesture all he wished to say. But Morris was trying to organise the elements of a noble ecstasy, grave yet with nothing in its eloquence to bring him shame, from an inner tract that had long since driven out all expressions of joy as a noisy nuisance.

'Oh I'm a bloody toff,' he moaned, circling with his head and pausing in the ante-rooms of rapture.

'You are that. You're a miracle.'

'You've done a lot for me.'

'Anything we can do to place a shield of comradely goodness between the teeth of the life urge and the rears of the subjects whom it seeks to favour with its special grip, we shall do.'

'God, it makes me feel funny, this suit.'

'It is making you feel, Morris, that you have come back from the deep waters of dark oceans to lands that have grown strange but lovelier to the eyes you bring from exile.'

'That's it, Walter. That's just how I feel. What d'you say? Dark oceans. That's where I've lived.' He squared his shoulders and put a new impulsive shape on his chin. 'I'm going to be worthy,' he said.

'Of whom? Of what?'

'Of this suit and Shadrach Sims.'

We raised our caps and bowed our heads towards the great bulge of Tudor Phelps' bowler. We were moved by a reverence that gurgled face downwards on the little lake of laughter into which the Terraces dipped their heart on nights of festival to keep it fresh. For our altar piece, the hat of that vanished nay-sayer, Tudor, struck us as being a brooding and more sardonic Buddha.

*****

After tea that evening we went for a stroll to the valley-bed. Many comrades came on to us and wanted our impressions of the day's working, even asking us to sign our autographs and write some little verse about the lifting of the shadow in their kids' copy books. Ben gave them a few short talks on paste and angles of sticking that were long remembered. Later in the evening, we were met by our friend Mr Simpson, the manager of the Exchange. He was coming out of one of the valley's large non-political clubs where the impulse to conserve waged fierce war on theory and reached a classic summary of its own quaint formulas in an endless routine of sitting, drinking, and card playing, seeking in an almost Trappist silence of mind and body an answer to the Celtic jape of always letting words pump the passionate fluid of his sadness into a vat of revolutionary intentions. Mr Simpson was merry and in a way to communicate. He closed one eye in a wink that expressed the essence of a genial evening in the club and an attractive desire to be at ease with the prolies and unbend in his off-moments. Mr Simpson was something of an entertainer and was well known as a chairman of concerts run by athletic clubs and groups of voters who liked their ideas small, monotonous and raw. Mr Simpson had a blue-nosed turn that kept these voters rolling.

'I bet you could tell me where Sims could stick his bills,' he said.

'Even there,' said Walter, 'we wouldn't be able to get them straight.'

137

'How is it going?'

'Dull but it does. We are going to keep at it, Mr Simpson. Save large sums, with Sims. If you want bills stuck, be they large or small, call. We advertise with brush and paste, all things chaste. If we do well with Shadrach he may be able to put us in the way of some regular work.'

'I don't think so.'

'Has he complained?'

'Not a word. But between us, Shadrach's future is not good. He's going on the rocks.'

'Honest?'

'Cross my club card. Sims is going to the wall. In his day he was a big, new unit and a lot of little men in front room shops found themselves locked in the back room when Shadrach and his cut prices came battering. Now it's his turn. There are newer and bigger units than his coming into the valley. They don't need to cut prices. They've got such a grip on supplies they just cut throats, Shadrach's for a start. So you see it's a grim life even for people who don't look like you. You are just the advance guard trying out the styles. You get a lot of nice people sharing the blade with you later on. There's something funny about Sims. He lacks stability. Ask any man who gets on and keeps on getting on what keeps him getting on and he'll say stability. But Sims is interested in something beyond groceries and that's green blight for a grocer. If he had stability he'd laugh at the notion of there being anything beyond groceries. If he wanted to keep his ground he'd have to be a deacon to keep in with the Christians and a muezzin, if he could get a copy of that shaky music, to get hold of any Arab trade that might come along. Instead of that he lives like a prince out in the country getting dreams, drink and women sent in by the crate and not quibbling about the empties. Now he wakes up to find his business taking its hat off the hook. He'll fight hard to keep it but it's too late. Soon he'll have to be giving up the Pontine. He's damned. But I don't think it'll matter to Shadrach. I think he's half mad. Good night and keep sticking as long as he keeps you supplied with anything to stick.'

'Well?' asked Arthur as soon as we were alone again.

'Shadrach is no half madder than we are,' said Walter.

'Perhaps Simpson would put us three quarters of the way. You don't know what standards these blokes accept.'

'Men like Simpson, who spend their time filling forms, stamping cards, looking for flaws, making rules, playing bowls and keeping neat, forget something. They forget that in our living quarters on this globe there is a large region of nightmare. I don't mean the nightmares that send our neighbours screaming around the bedroom after cheese or around the house after their best friends. I mean great multitudes of people who can't shake off the notion that they do not know what this life is all about and keep crying out for a handbook. They want to know what they were awakened for in the first place and who had the cheek to set them to marching about in this parade of growing, working and wondering. It's no joke being mixed up with these antics. They are the trapped ones and they can't even have the consolation of trapped animals who may know that soon the trapper will come along, lift the spring, end the agony and do himself a bit of good by selling the skin for a profit. To express these feelings they take a good look at the life pattern around them, the many and curious ways in which men shape up to and bristle at each other and prepare to play hell with themselves. Then they take a good kick at the pattern and the relationships in their area, start grunting and rushing about, issuing decrees, filling up County Court orders and the County Court as well, proving they are every bit as frightened as the poor sod who did the kicking and trying to get back as fast as possible to the spot they were kicked from. We boys are not only in the Terraces. We are also in a tug of war. If you ever find your two legs very far apart for no reason that you know and aching like hell it is this tug of war, so don't worry. We are in the middle of two long ropes of death made sharp and cutting by the tempered tomfoolery of fears we use to keep the strands tight. We have to be harder than our fathers' fears not to have these ropes cut us to tatters. Shadrach's a nightmare man. He's out to play hell.'

'Put sand in the sugar and wheel grease in the marge, you mean?'

'Nothing so petty. Shadrach's been an outlaw for a long time. Being an outlaw isn't just being ugly, shot at, hanged and paid a reward on. It's being in a world that is genuinely puzzling, a world angry with the smart of not being understood and bitterly keen on working out new sets of puzzles to worry the voters hairless. Shadrach does well out of business and roysters in a place that demands that all successful traders be registered apostles of the Lord. He isn't like those bankers' darlings who untie their bales around these valleys and prove their virtue by tip-toeing away from life in its redder patches and pretend it's something that has just slipped in through a crack in the tiles and will be swept away in the morning. Shadrach wants the proof of life within himself as well as in the faces of the people whom he serves, swindles and uses as boiling pieces in his stew of surplus value. The wealthy pious hate the lusting untidiness of his appetites. It threatens the whole current of thrift, caution and thought for one's good name that silts up the desires of the poor and helps keep their grocery bills paid. But Shadrach is failing. The wall has been built and his head is being lowered for grinding into it. The alliance of money and cant will make a mincemeat of Shadrach and he will join us in the shadow after he has sent in his formal request that we move up and make room. These things have to be done with proper ceremony. From now on the fear will start rising in him like the mist does when heat and cold start staring at each other. Betrayal above and hatred from below will rot his foundations. When he begins to totter he will seize at every instrument, person or event that will give him a deeper sense of his own being, a sense of talking right out at life in a fine flashing series of damns and blasts and not having life breathing into his ear its horrible sentences of ridicule, banishment or death. As for ourselves having no future with Shadrach, I smile. It is good to see the same sharp scythe of undirected change moving towards his body as it moved long since through ours. We are a bright bloody lot of clover and the heap is getting higher all the time.'

We walked up to the Terraces and upon the face of our friend Walter was the look of fascinated compassion which it always wore when he felt the creative movements of his own dark fancy finding sister rhythms in the forces that churn the scum of our experience into the smiles of the strong and the whimpers of the feeble who fail and fall with their notion of the truth still clutched between their fingers.

*****

Shadrach came to see us again the following day. We thought it queer that he should come to see us, the least significant of all his retainers. As he watched us, we caught more strongly from his expression and gestures the sense of distraction in which solitude walked with an almost personal identity, conscious, militant and menacing. Often we found him staring up at the gaunt skeleton of streets that formed the Terraces and stained the hillside. His unease seemed to find something to feed on in the sight of them.

'Oh bloody bloody...' he said. 'I'd like to burn the whole damned issue. I shake inside at the sight of it. There's nothing worse than the unfit in a state of half-oppression. It puts a curb on oppressed and oppressor. We get nowhere. The man who quiesces in a life of half-starvation degrades himself and the very feel of life for others. He's a slug. He would be ennobled and dignified by a course of brutal violence because that would be life taking notice of him and speeding up the daft programme of not being dead.' He turned away from us and lay down on the soft green patch of grass near the wall where we were supposed to be working. 'Trouble with me,' he said. 'I'm not like other men. No, that's daft. Not much like other men. Stillness in any shape or form gives me the itch.'

We nodded. We believe strongly in flattering the life-illusion of all voters who pass it on to us. It is not often we do this for most of the people we know have had a long course in advanced reality on the Social Insurance and are only small holders in this matter of delusion. We were surprised to see how lithe and powerful the body of Shadrach was. There was something tightly malevolent in the shape of his head and neck.

'Sometimes,' he said, 'it's good to be like other men. I'll say something to you blokes. Silly of me to be saying anything of the sort to types like you but you look no more human to me than that wall or those clouds. You'll hear the words of what I say. The meaning will go the same way as my breath or the smoke of this cigarette. You know old Nichols, the man who owns most of the other grocery shops in this part of the valley? He came to see me today, grey-haired, neat and stooping with holiness. Shadrach, he said, you lack a proper respect for the old ideas of loyalty and discipline. There's a spiritual side to trade that you've missed and it's a big comfort. What devil is in you, Shadrach, he asked, and he put his clean thin fingers near me as if he wanted to be at grips with this devil and drag the thing forth. I pushed him away but he only smiled. He is obedient to life, that grim and ancient bastard. He'll never hear anything out of tune because he never heard any tune to start with. He said I was going to pot and heading for the coop because the Christian wrath of the people was turning against me, me being a well known goat and not given to talking over the fence with the faithful. It's a wonder a fissure doesn't open in the earth to draw away old sods who

143

talk such stuff as that. He said, Shadrach, you ought to marry. My daughter, Jennifer, he said, is a fine upstanding steady girl. She's like a framed text, that Jennifer, and she whistles the Dead March from Saul at you every time you look at her, crooking her fingers to make them look like a bier and clicking her teeth to tap out the rhythm. And she paralyses you when she does that because she grows to look steadier and more upstanding with every note and all you can do is wait for the boom-boom part and sing it out loud. When the Creative Will begins its journey through these Terraces, these catacombs, there will be a phase of wonderful wickedness among the new leaders. When men consent to whimper, somebody with the urge to kick them to an even higher note will hurt their bodies till they scream. What the devil am I doing selling food to people when I'd much rather see them dead. Don't answer. Who the hell are you to be fathoming such mysteries? Carry on with your bill sticking. Your stroke is just clumsy enough to make me feel divine... You remember that lad Watts?'

'We remember him, Mr Sims.'

'I've seen him. He's raw, a little ignorant but full of strength and passion. I've had a few chats with him. He's beginning to get my drift. He talks badly. I want you men to do something for me. You said you agreed with my views about this valley, didn't you?'

'Anything you say, Mr Sims. You can stick your notions on to us like we stick your bills on to walls.'

'I've taken over that large disused millinery store in the main street. I'm having it done out as a Youth Club for games and discussion. Watts can prepare himself there to take a

144

lead. In the meantime, he'll have to learn to talk better. As he is now any little Trade Union official or Moscow pimp would make him look a fool. I've arranged for him to spend a few evenings a week in a small room behind that shop explaining his ideas to you chaps and putting some point on them. It won't be for nothing. I'll make it worth your while. Listening to Watts in his present state is hard labour. Give him some hints on what you think will get under people's skin, canny little barbs that will prick even their inertia and make them want to strangle the shabby-minded radical illiterates who paunch around promising them lives of golden ease once they've thrown aside their natural leaders. The poor have achieved so little that once you can make them hate that achievement you have their heart in your hand and you can do with it what you please. They become sick with the sense of betrayal only when it is one of their brothers who does the betraying. Strengthen them in that weakness and we will soon have them ready to tear the skin from all who do not reject offhand the swindle of brotherhood. Rollo still doesn't know how easy it is to keep this species mad, split and screaming.'

'The trouble with Rollo,' said Walter simply, 'is love.'

'What are you talking about?' asked Shadrach, sharply, as if amazed that an opinion could come from our quarter. 'His love for himself, you mean? Nothing wrong with that. That's part of the Creative Will.'

'No, love for a girl. A sort of love we have seen doing more damage to the voters than rats to an embankment. Rollo has a girl, Clarisse. Every time he sees her he looks like the furnaces in Port Talbot at opening time. He gapes, glows and belches flame then turns his ears up to have Clarisse scrape out the pig iron.'

'Well?'

'This devotion has no doubt curdled the wits of Rollo and is making his propaganda thick and hard to follow.'

'What do you suggest? That we geld Rollo? That may sound good sense to you but I am only a grocer and not a high priest with powers of off or on in this particular. In any case I have a bias towards the flesh myself.'

'But Rollo's task here is not going to be an easy one. The voters here have gone hungry in strikes for months on end trying to persuade their natural leaders to go somewhere else and lead. They will not take kindly to anyone who talks to them of the rule of the strong for that rule has been cuffing them hard behind the ear every time they've put their ear out of doors. They also believe in equality but that is probably a complaint brought on by lack of proper food and not having enough blankets on the bed. If they were kept fat and drowsy I don't think they'd make an issue out of it. In view of all these difficulties we think Rollo should be free to concentrate on his mission.'

'Quite right. Just pass the stuff you just told me on to Rollo. That's the local human material he'll need.'

'Thank you, Mr Sims. And another thing. This girl, Clarisse, has a great admiration for you.'

'Is that so?'

'She has told us of this admiration. She has told us that you are a man to sway the nation if you did not have so much of a poet's heart.'

'Good God! How exactly right that is! If she had been

curled up inside my mind she would not have known me better. What's this girl's name?'

'Clarisse Harris.'

'What else did she say?'

'Many things. In the eye and the utterance of Mr Sims, she said, there is power. There is no doubt that she has to do with this Rollo, young and raw as he is, only because she hears in him an echo of yourself. I don't think you could have any idea, Mr Sims, of the esteem in which you are held by the women and girls of the Terraces. But the esteem of this Clarisse is in a class of its own.'

'The girl sounds uncanny. What does she look like?'

'She has a big welcoming body. In her eyes there is all the wisdom of one who has rejected the democratic myth. She was helped in that by her father who has been bitter ever since he failed to get a job with the Council. And on her lips you see the promise of mind going down like a skittle at the slightest touch of heat near the glands.'

'Yes, she may cure the sadness of my nights. I have been lonely and inwardly sick ever since I came back to the valley. I want a change of flavour and a change of sky. It will do Watts good to be without this Clarisse for a change. He is not a strong-looking type. If she is the sort of girl you describe, too rich for the blood, he will be doing his speaking through a tube coming up from the tomb or held up on steel props and confusing the voters by asking for two oysters as well as acres with every cow. Bring her to me.'

*****

147

Later that day we called at the shop where Clarisse, the young widow had found work. She did a short dance when she heard that Mr Sims would like to see her about some special work in connection with the Creative Will. It was clear that Shadrach had carved an even deeper notch on her impressions than Rollo. There was a ripe comeliness in the blend of thick body and costly suitings of Shadrach and a fascination for the young in the shadows which he flung into his face and his words.

'I think Mr Sims is the most wonderful man in all this valley. He is flesh among dry bones.' She flashed her eyes at us in a purposeful way as she said that and we tried to look as moist as we could and moved closer to each other to reduce the tell-tale rattle. 'I shall do this special work with glee.'

'But don't tell Rollo.'

'Why not, for discipline's sake?'

'Rollo is an artist. His art lies in changing the lives of others, charging our soil with a new richness so that our dreams can grow a new suit of evergreen combinations, intending no coarseness. He's keen on you. He will ponder over seeing you with Mr Sims. No good propaganda and only a few straggly fragments of Creative Will ever came out of men who ponder. There must be no shadows in Rollo's head. We've already got a stock of shadows of our own better than anything outside the place where they actually make night.'

'All right then.' We could see her Creative Will unbending as her mind slipped down into a giggling excitement. 'Rollo won't mind a few white lies.'

'Not unless you give them to him in volume form or do the bleaching in front of him. We are to help Rollo with his platform work. We are the platform. He'll be too busy for a while to do anything but lay the foundation of a resurrected valley.'

That same day we began our evenings as sounding boards for Rollo. Shadrach had not yet got the electric current switched into the millinery shop and we sat in the small back room with an oil lamp on the table. We sat on one side, looking intent and, if the looker were not accustomed to the curious pallor that can be reached by mixing together a complete social disaster, some acute thinking about same and the light of a short-wicked oil lamp, sinister. Rollo, at first, was arrogant and fixed us with a stare that was as assured as sunlight as he tried to enlarge on the brief doctrinal notes he had received from Shadrach and to remove from our faces the occasional expression they wore of having no great pride in being white, aryan or even human. It was hard work for us to put up with Rollo, harder even than the bare chairs we sat on. But the eyes of our friend Walter counselled patience. As a speaker he was little better than the first ape who found out that he could get things just as fast by asking as by stretching and started off oratory in that way. As for his treatment of ideas, he would take a thought, growl at it like a dog at a porcupine as if trying to bully the thing into taking in its bristles, then tear the widest hell out of it without getting an inch nearer its centre and its meaning. When passionate conviction swung an arm to cut a swathe through the thicket of his tiny theories he rocked, writhing through a great arc of frothing excitement. He became no clearer. We even tried keeping our ears on the table to see if the vibrations would help us follow his zagging track more clearly but this got us nowhere save on to the table and into Rollo's bad books since he thought the gesture meant we were dropping off under the strain and being frank about it. And our anger as he spoke in twisting, fierce stupid phrases about the people among whom we lived, our people, us, rose swiftly up into every last corner of our being and pressed painfully against all the places of exit. Most nights Ben had to crouch behind the table and strap his arm to his knee or come in with his hand done up in a sling to prevent him from pushing away the table and crowning Rollo, with his fist or the table. But Rollo suffered no less than we, when we began, coolly and without pity, to comb the hair upon his ancient fallacies and to reveal to him, as wrath dragged him through one impotent, inarticulate spasm after another, the basic bog of quaking foolishness in which his childish snobberies pecked their way and stretched their necks to crow. It was then that he banged his books and his notes on the table and moaned for Clarisse to give him some comfort.

'She's got an aunt ill to the point of death,' he explained. 'She can't see me. Just at the time when Mr Sims asks you blokes to sit here with me and drive me mad. You try to pick holes in what I say. You think you know better than I do. What game are you shabby loons supposed to be playing? If I say a thing, it's right. And one day when I say a thing you won't have any chance of telling me it all depends on the class angle or some damned nonsense like that. You'll like it or lump it.'

150

'We're only trying to help, Rollo,' said Walter. 'Your ideas are bound to triumph. But the voters in these Terraces have things going on in their heads that they take for truth. You know how you mistake people in the dark? It's the same with thoughts. They are bound to ask you questions when you begin to treat of such issues as wages or food vouchers, work or no work, capitalism or socialism, groceries or grass, the family or the stud, because they are at the receiving end of all these issues. So you mustn't mind if we heckle.'

'You're obstinate and sometimes I think you're laughing at me.'

'Laughing? God, no. It's the flicker of the lamp on our faces.'

'I hope so. I won't stand any nonsense from you sods.'

We could see he missed Clarisse gravely. We have been told that in this business of the flesh some women lead men to high pastures, a fullness of delight that competes in completeness with death itself. And from that moment the lungs of their longing shrink and bring them a bitter pain whenever they do not breathe the air of the old fulfilment. Clarisse, it was evident, had led Rollo by way of a twisting goat path to some high summit and between the anguish of his present banishment and our gnawing attempt to hollow a pit of doubting beneath him he had come to a point where we could feel his frustration shudder around the room like a dancer.

'I've had enough of this. You blokes strike me as being in league with the enemy. What you need is barbed wire in double thickness around those prying bloody minds of yours. I'm going to see Mr Sims. I've had enough of this part of the course.'

'I agree, Rollo,' said Walter. 'You're ready, boy. He asked me to tell you to come along and see him any time you have something of importance to tell him. "Tell him to come and not to bother to knock." That's what he said. "I may be dozing and I do not want Rollo to wait. Rollo has big things to do. I think the world of Rollo." That's just a sample of the sort of things Mr Sims thinks of you.'

The praise brought a little of the old glowing serenity back into Rollo's face. He studied himself in a small hand mirror he took from his waistcoat pocket and shook out in a single gesture which we thought very nimble his greased curls and the pleats of his golfing knickers.

We left the building and made our way down the main street. We padded behind Rollo, smoothly performing our role of footmen to the fates, committee men to the life urge.

Rollo walked up the stairs that led to Shadrach's flat. I do not think he knew we were behind him. The gravity of his own existence had made him insensitive to his fellows. Rollo could have been quite alone on this earth for ten years before noticing that things were rather quiet. He opened the door. On a divan at the further end of the room, lit by a lamp of heavy design and controlled brilliance, were Shadrach and the girl Clarisse, close to each other and shaping up for some phase of further closeness in a way that struck us at first sight as laughable but which we have been told is usual among those who follow this carnality as a means of expression. Rollo said not a word. Then he began to vibrate like a motor. The last link of his restraint, worn thin by the teeth of our patient malice, was snapping. We observed, when not counting the beat of Rollo's vibrations to keep a check on tempo, that the lips of the girl Clarisse were drawn away from her teeth, giving her the look of a stoat. We could not see Shadrach's teeth, crane and twist as we might, but the rest of him had the look of a man who has a fancy for, and a way with, stoats. We could feel the indecision flutter in Rollo. His being was founded upon a worship of men like Shadrach. Our friend Walter slipped forward and closed the door. Between us we hurried Rollo to the foot of the stairs. We walked him along the pavement. We held him firm, with just the right degree of strength to suggest a disciplined pity. We could hear the words coming up from inside him deadened to a far rumble by the lava that coated them.

'Be strong, Rollo,' said Walter. 'You stand for strength against our weakness. Do not show yourself to us in weakness. This is our time of trial and preparation. Who is this Clarisse compared with your mission? Mr Sims himself told us no woman should be allowed to nibble at the Creative Will or any other part of a natural leader. Enjoy these women if nature bids you so to do but keep your heart whole in position for the great fight.'

Rollo made no reply. He walked with us up into the Terraces. We paused to let him sit on one of the many benches the Council in its kindness had planted here and there to ease the cruelty of our slopes. Rollo laid his head on the cold rain-studded woodwork of the seat's back. The great mass of the Terraces, showing its long ribs of gaslight was all around us.

'The sound of her, full of song as it may seem now, will die from your heart,' said Walter in a voice that was a shadow dipped in grieving. 'She was sent to beat your metal to a fine point. Think of these people around us here, crouched in their craven darkness waiting for the bugle of Rollo Watts to lead them out into a new age of dignified firmness, through obedience. Your destiny, Rollo, cuts you off from the feebleness and folly of us who are the passive tools of greater wills than ours.'

Rollo stared down at the street from which he had come. There was such a debate going on inside him we could almost hear the chairman giving his lust the floor. Then he gave his curls and pleats another of those swift double-purpose shakes.

'I'm all right,' he said quietly. 'She's nothing.'

'We have never,' said my friend Walter, 'been prouder of Rollo Watts than we are at this moment.'

Rollo left us and branched rightwards to the part of the Terraces where he lived.

'Walter,' said Arthur. 'Many times I have listened to you with admiration. Often on the mud that had blocked our stream your wisdom has traced patterns of white and thoughtful loveliness. But for depth and consistency you have done nothing to beat the programme of sheer flat-headedness you have been palming off on Sims and this Rollo. What are you trying to prove. That we have reached a stage of confusion where truth and its opposite can play the fool and nip into each other's clothes at will? Or that one needs to be wise to be the inspiration of an idiot in an age when idiocy is so usual and established as not to be inspiring?'

154

'Compassion is my country,' said Walter. 'In all living things there is one point which we can touch and share the current of thought and feeling that nourishes their hidden life. To do this and yet avoid the wastage of a general sightless pity, that's the job.'

'In all living things? Even in those who are little more than the walking reasons of our defeat and discomfort?'

'Even, at times, in them.'

'It'll come,' said Ben.

'What'll come?' I asked, seeing from the distant look on Ben's face that he did not mean to add anything to this immediate talk on the currents that keep the hidden life in motion. Ben had little patience with forces that needed to be guessed. He thought the going was hard enough with only the things that were very visible around us.

'The day,' said Ben, 'when I, as my friend Walter said, will beat the metal of this Rollo to a finer point. The point will be so fine he'll be able to keep the rain off with a postage stamp. So he will not need to catch cold when we post him off for cleaning.'

*****

It was a few days later that we saw Morris again. He came into sight as we were on our way down the Terraces to collect our last bundles of bills from Shadrach. He had already enlarged twice the limits of the territory we were to cover but even so, we expected that day to be the last of our professional connection with him. There was a limit to the walls and boards on which bills could be stuck and a limit to the number of people who were willing to put up with the sight and sound of us coming around trying to prove to them that their future lay with Sims and trying to look as if we believed this. Morris stepped around a corner and appeared suddenly before us as if he had been on the watch and waiting for us. He was still mauved to the point of collapse in that stomachic herb mixture of a suit. On his head he still wore the gigantic hat of the dead Tudor Phelps who had seen no wrong in death. The bowler looked more than ever like a small sable hill above his pale short frame. But a change had fallen upon Morris. There was a liveliness in his eye and a reasoned purpose in his smile. His smile in the past had been a functionless grimace meant, not to show pleasure or teeth but simply to prove to himself and the other voters that he still had the power to move his own face if not anything else in the area. We stopped to greet him. He raised his arm to rivet our attention. We gave it the rivet for we had no intention of rushing our work that day. The emotion of waking up and finding we had somewhere to go from bed had worn thin. In any case, Morris was as worth watching as any sunset in his present garb. He was, against the background of an average Terrace, that very Beulah land to which we had likened his daughter on the day of her ascension. He did not say anything. He pulled a small note book from his inside pocket. Then from his breast pocket he took a pencil. He held these two articles up for us to view them as if they were beads, he a missionary and we a league of dogmatic pagans given to eating all white envoys when not distracted by these gauds. We drew closer. We had never seen such signs of culture in

Morris before. He held the note book in his hand, open. He raised the pencil to his lips and began to wet it, with an enjoyment that made us think he was only waiting for something to take the hardness and blackness from the lead before putting the whole pencil in his mouth and beginning to chew. He was trying, through these antics, to convey some message to us, some bit of news that had filled him with such delight, the usual instruments of feeling and telling had grown cheap, brittle, not to be trusted. At first we thought that these gestures might be some insane charade brought on by the shock of his suit, with the pencil and paper meant to convey that with Morris setting the pace in glory for the entire Terraces, he should now be written up as a part of history. We agreed. In any time or place, Morris, as he looked then, would have merited a stone tablet, fixed right above him and limiting his movements to such jobs as haunting. Ben entered into the spirit of Morris' game. Ben had no note book but he dipped his brush into the paste and began writing with it on the air that stood between him and Morris. Morris stepped back and shouted to Ben to be careful with the paste which might fly towards his suit.

'Speak up, Morris,' said Arthur. 'What are you itching to tell us, boy? Have you just learned to write or have you sold off one of your kids for a pencil.'

'I'm one of you now,' said Morris. His voice was confident, as if beginning a litany.

'On the paste, you mean?' asked Ben. 'Shadrach must be branching out.'

'No. I've got a job once a week.'

157

'Preaching?' asked Walter. There was nothing mysterious in that suggestion. Many sects in the valley had been founded on departures from the normal less clamant than the stripes in Morris' suit. We could well imagine him being taken up by the less balanced voters as the year's most potent symbol.

'No. Collecting the dues from people in the top Terrace who are in Shadrach Sims' Food Club. Very slow to pay, those boys in the top Terrace. They're so high up they forget about laws. Sims said the sight of me done up like this would sober them no end.'

'It will, boy. Those people in the top Terrace would be singing another tune if they knew you were coming.'

'They would, that. This suit has done something for me. I know now that I've been rescued from the grave. I know now that I'm going to get on. There's strength welling up in me. I went and told Shadrach these things. He looked at me. He said he bet the grave was wild and stamping at missing me because it had been a near thing with me looking so bleached and good for nothing in The Days Before The Suit. So he gave me the addresses of a lot of people in the top Terraces so deep in his debt they got to climb up if they want more food. I'm going to get them to renew their clubs. He said if they looked a bit surprised to see me when they opened the door this surprise was no more than a kind of hunger pang and it would be cured by any of the many titbits that can be found in the Shadrach Sims One Pound Hamper.' He brought out his note book again with a quick jerk of the arm. He had been practising. 'How would you blokes like to start clubbing in? You look as if you could do with a hamper.'

158

'No thank you, Morris. We eat by the moon. When it's full, so are we. We are glad to see you so set on getting on.'

'You blokes will be amazed at the speed I'll get on. Shadrach's got his eye on me and anybody Shadrach's got his eye on, shoots on like a bullet. By the time I finish I'll make that Eurona sorry.'

'Eurona? Sorry for what?'

'Sorry she ever gave me the worry and trouble she did over those clothes. Look at the turn she gave me, putting me in fear of losing my Insurance and making me duck every time I saw a man who looked as if he might be coming around for the Government. And I'll make her sorry too for the way she looks at me. She stays there in the house and never goes out, looking at me as if I were to blame, as if I had told her to put those clothes on the fire.'

'That's right, Morris. You make her sorry. You make everybody sorry. It's as good a programme as you'll ever think of, timely and to the point and you're the boy and that's the suit to carry it out. Spread sorrow over the bloody place like snow and we'll all pad over it silent like wolves, wailing the songs of solitude to the beat of nibs rattled in a skull by the boys at the Ministry of Labour.'

Morris looked defiantly at our friend Walter. There was none of the distrust or bemusement that had filled his face before on hearing one of Walter's elegies on human relations.

'What you need, Walter,' he said in a brisk, almost bourgeois tone, 'is a night on the tiles and a suit.'

When next we saw Shadrach, Walter bowed at him from the middle. We found this manoeuvre strange, even against the background of obscure trafficking that Walter was doing with Shadrach, Rollo and the young widow. But we bowed with him all the same. There was rare harmony of line and timing in our movements. We looked like a male voice party newly landed from Japan.

'What are you up to now?' asked Shadrach.

'We salute you for Morris.'

'Why should Morris need saluting for?'

'That suit made a new man of him, Mr Sims.'

'He needed remaking. That man was making a mock of nature. Once get nature a bad name and the bottom falls out of more things than the grocery trade.'

'It was wonderful.'

'The least I could do.'

'As far as we here in the Terraces are concerned I have been delegated to tell you that it was the biggest thing since Genesis.'

'I'm a man who likes changing things.'

'News of Morris and his new outlook, his hunger to get on and be at grips with the life force is spreading fast through the Terraces and putting your name on the lips of voters who have been too depressed to talk for a decade. It's a revelation of what one strong man can do if he has the will. We knew Morris for many years as a man who always hung on to the wall whenever the road sweepers came around, having seen many of his friends, bleached to an even lighter shade than his own, vanish from the bin into the cart. He was less than the dust but slighter and not yet set to music. He was lower in the scale of death than Lazarus or Howell the Good and now he is purple from head to foot in this splendid suit, looking keener than any hawk, flashing out that note book like a gun and using a pencil like a clerk on behalf of your food clubs. The Terraces would not have been more surprised if all this had happened to Eurona.'

'Eurona?'

'Morris' daughter.'

'What's the matter with her?'

We all shook our heads in time with Walter. We wore looks of the blackest misery as if, in this matter of describing the plight of Eurona, we would need at least a month to find the beginnings of a formula.

'Well?' asked Shadrach, annoyed. 'What's the matter with her? Has she got the same grey squalid look her old man put on?'

'Worse than Morris.'

'Can't be done. He took some swallowing, that Morris. But when I accepted him as genuine I decided there and then that two-legged life could go no lower than Morris. He is the Southern pole of life, discoloured, warped and worn to a short stump. That man is either on or under the flagstones.'

'But you should see Eurona. She's really terrible. She's Morris' masterpiece. Morris was only mixing his shades in the palette on himself and working out the rough idea and outline. With Eurona he got down to it. The Government has seen her but they'll have to pass a new Act before they can believe her. Every time she stands up straight her clothes fall off.'

'What about her? Are you trying to sell me the magic word that'll make her stand up straight?'

'Eurona, Mr Sims, is a kind of test case in these Terraces. In the hope or despair we see upon her face we find a kind of barometer of life and death in these Terraces. If she were to be restored to confidence and beauty through your aid, the Terraces would be confirmed in their belief in you as the seller not of good food only but as the prophet of a new day. She is a pretty girl, this Eurona.' Walter put in here a short sketch of Eurona, the elusive, misty-morning beauty of her face and frame, the naive devotion of her character, but making no mention of Rollo, the grant, the clothes, the climax and our present unease with regard to the foxhunter and the regulations of the Government.

'And she thinks the world of you, Mr Sims,' added Walter.

'Does she now?'

'She's heard about you from her old man. If ever you want your feet kissed, Mr Sims, just give this girl a fresh start, then take off your boot.'

'She's young, you say. Very important point that. It's of the highest value that a new attitude should be inspired in these young people who've never seen their parents go out to work except in the toilet.'

'The highest value. The key to the whole question.'

'You say she's ragged?'

'She's pagan, next door to naked.'

'Well, that's one thing we can repair anyway. Anybody who thinks the world of Shadrach Sims deserves to be properly covered.' He wrote out another of those magical notes. 'Give that to Morris. Tell him to get the girl what she needs within reasonable limits. At the store where he got that suit and leave the choice of colour to her, because Morris seems gone on purple. Then I'll see what can be done for her. I've got a poet's mind and a sculptor's hands. I pinch away at life. You'd be surprised at the shapes that come up between my fingers when the clay is soft enough.'

We went on our way.

'Tell me, Walter,' said Arthur. 'According to the version of history that you are now presenting for some good end which you know and we don't, is there any female in this division, woman or girl, outside of that very old and bitter woman Angela Hancock who left her relatives and went to live full time with her chickens, who does not think the world of Shadrach Sims?'

'There's not a woman about whom Shadrach would not be willing to believe that. You'll notice about these two, Shadrach and Rollo, both tortured by the sense of being unique and with a strong down on equality in any shape or form, with whom we are now having to do, that they both have a demented notion of their own value. Until knowledge can show us the gland which, made smaller here or larger there, can bring these types back to the ordinary run, we have to keep our eyes open for such performers. Such men are weeds and in the soil of the rich, organised misery we have here there would be abundant growth for them once root had been struck in the more corrupt and hopeless clods of jealousy and spite. You would have to be a genius to find any bit of praise to give either of these two that they had not already given to themselves. Before their wholesome breakfasts in the morning they stand before a mirror for a long formal round of congratulations. That is why it is so easy for us, who feed on the frozen field of doubt and self-hatred where events have hedged us in, to

163

deceive them and that is why it is so easy for them who love themselves with a love that knows no hedge or bound to destroy us who seem to doubt the reasons for that love.'

*****

That afternoon, we saw Rollo. He was sitting on a bench at the terminus of a bus route that operated along a long cleft in the valleyside. He shared the bench with the driver of the bus in which he served as conductor. This driver's name was Ivor, a short, thick man, without joy, made more morose by stomach trouble. Ivor was a man who spoke little and that little showed in every syllable how sourly unpleased he was with himself, buses and the world in which they moved and in which he worked to help a stomach which he hated to live, all at the order of inherited and compulsive duties which struck Ivor as being as much in need of magnesia as he was. We could see that between Ivor and Rollo there was no link except the bus company and the air. Ivor took out a bag of sandwiches, ineptly cut and thick as the wood of the bench. He began to chew through one of these sandwiches with the speed and thoroughness of a mechanical scoop. We grew to wonder as we watched. It was not odd, we thought, that Ivor's stomach was bad. It was only odd that it had not been driven to take shelter with a neighbour until Ivor had blown over. Rollo ate nothing and watched Ivor's champing with disgust.

'There'll be a day of reckoning for goats like him,' said Rollo in a whisper to Walter.

Arthur and Ben sat down on the bench by Ivor and

began talking about man's stomach about which Arthur had written the draft of a poem in black stanzas. Walter and I stood near Rollo. He was worried and fidgety.

'You remember my friend Clarisse Harris?' he asked.

'Yes. We remember. A fine upstanding girl, Miss Harris.'

'She was. She has gone to Cardiff to live. Mr Sims is taking a keen interest in her and has found her a job in the city which will give her a better future. She always said that she would never find her proper field of work here. Now she has gone.'

He fell silent. We could see that the going of Clarisse had drawn a long tough root of feeling from Rollo. We could see too that his mind was in conflict on the subject of Shadrach Sims. It was clear that Rollo in this momentary frustration was beginning to perceive the outline of that humility, born of resentment ripening into panic, which is the trade mark of those masses who are the raw material of our crises, the material that gets rawer all the time.

'Mr Sims knows best,' said Walter. 'Now you will be free to grow.'

'Grow what?'

'Yourself. Politics and the love-passion together in our hearts shake it too much and tear the fabric. Men like you must either be alone or with women who love you humbly, quietly and bring their own oxygen.'

'You read that in the Sunday paper.'

'I don't read on Sunday. My brother comes and takes his glasses back so he can read the Sunday paper. That Clarisse was the wrong girl for you, Rollo. You need a girl who belongs to the Terraces. The people would think more of you

165

seeing you favour a girl they know, some girl who walks around in a drab and neglected state that makes her a bronze monument to the rotting errors of freedom and democratic equality. That girl Eurona Morris for a start.'

'Oh yes, I remember her. I went about with her for a few nights. But the last time I saw her she was looking clean and fresh.'

'She's been drawn through the chimney since then. Morris has not yet heard of the law that abolished human brushes for the soot. Those few nights she had with you were golden drops in her sad life, Rollo. That girl is abject at the mention of your name.'

'I suppose she is. She still about?'

'Still here and I bet she'd betray her old man to the Philistines for another word with you.'

'I suppose she would. There's a lot in what you say. For a man like me, it's a woman's fidelity is all he needs. Dog-like fidelity,' Rollo gave a short whistle, snapped his fingers and slapped his knee, to show the way he had with dogs.

'That's right,' said Walter. 'Dog-like fidelity. And Eurona's your dog. If you want a lead, we'll boil Morris down until we reach the leather.'

*****

When we came home that evening, Morris was waiting for us. 'Come with me,' he said, standing still, looking sombre and using a tone so hushedly reverent we thought at first he had said: 'Abide with me,' and we imagined he had now, having reached the stage of speaking only in a hush and hymn titles, finished off the job of becoming lunatic.

166

He took us to his house. On the threshold he paused and said: 'Sims has done it again.'

We followed him into the front room of the house. There were many persons in the room and this for a moment hid the fact that there was nothing but persons in the room. It was bare. Eurona stood in the middle of a ring made up of her sisters and friends brought in from the houses around by the excited vibrations of Morris and his family. Eurona was dressed in finery similar in colour and cut to that she had bought the time before. Even the Fixo and the face powder had been put into position. We showed our great pleasure at her new beauty. She came up to us as soon as she saw us enter, smiled and pressed our hands, thinking, no doubt, that it was once more to our skill in playing on human weaknesses and playing conjuring tricks with the Government that she owed this last shipment of the incredible. The friends fell back a little, dismayed, believing from our pensive look that we had surely come to denounce somebody or taking something back to the shop. Walter took Eurona to one side.

'Go to the street where Rollo lives about the time he comes off work. He needs you, Eurona. He has had a deep hurt. You can give him comfort. Do not tax him with his conduct with the widow.' Our friend Walter sounded as if he were reading from a recipe book and we would not have liked to look at the cover to see what the recipe was for. 'Be fond and forgiving. What he needs is the simple affection of a mother from someone who is not his mother.'

Her eyes glowed and we could see her tears softening the bright green of them. She pressed our hands again with a pride and a passion of thankfulness that gave us pain.

167

'Didn't I always tell you?' she said. 'Didn't I always say that my love was like a flower, that it would find the light however deep the earth above it, that it would be like this?'

We looked hard at her, thinking many things, but mainly of how easy it is to squeeze great jets of either gratitude or daftness from men and women, and by antics so clumsy they make you turn away with shame, for yourself and for those who give their stupidity or their thanks.

*****

'He was there,' said Morris. 'In the porch with my Eurona.'

'Who was there?'

'That Rollo. One of the best catches in the Terraces. Have you seen those knickers? Have you ever felt that black poke on his cap. I'm not saying they're anywhere up to the standard of my suit but they give him a very smart look.'

'Where were you?'

'In the passage, listening.'

'I hope they spoke clear.'

'Like bells. I heard every word. Rollo was telling my Eurona how sorry he was he had ever taken up with the widow. But he didn't get to that part for a long time. For half an hour at least he spoke in a proud way, talking about his future and giving facts and figures showing the wealth of the bus company. That part of it was very interesting to me too because it's the sort of information that will make an impression on Shadrach Sims next time I talk with him. He ended up by saying that he would be faithful to Eurona for ever and ever.'

'I can't see how your kids can fail with you taking down the dialogue like this.'

'This is a happy day for me.'

Morris broke away from us to announce an end to gloom in some other Terrace. We went and sat on our wall. There Eurona came for a brief chat to thank us once more for all we had done.

'Don't thank us, Eurona,' said Walter. 'You know who got you those clothes?' We nodded to say no when she pointed at us.

'My father then. So that's why he looked so knowing when he brought the voucher and took me down to the store. He didn't say anything. So it was him after all. He always said he would make something of himself once he had a suit that was all the same colour and a hat like Tudor Phelps. Now he's a man to bargain with.'

'Your old man, Eurona, is in himself, a bargain. No, those clothes came from Shadrach Sims, one of the greatest names in this valley. He has known of you for a long time, Eurona, has pitied you, as we have, and known of your dreams. He is far above Rollo as that mountain is above us. And Shadrach Sims wishes to bring you out of all this darkness. He wishes to help you, Eurona, to stand between you and the world and put into its words the language of your longings. He wants to give back to you in golden measure the strength that has been robbed from you by the shame and dirt that have grown around you in these Terraces. He will ask you to come to him. He wishes to speak to you, to teach you to walk through the snows that crown the tall summits of your hunger. When you go to see

169

him, he will show you pity. But don't forget that behind the pity there will be the beginnings of love.'

Ben began waving his cap to clear the air. Eurona's eyes reached a peak of illumination. We could see that the moods of ecstasy and escape had grown to a point where she would advance boldly to seize any food that would speed her growth, any light of given love that would strengthen her gait. She was a vessel perfectly shaped and hollowed by privation's longest teeth for the reception of love in any form or on any plane. The amount, quality and location would depend only on the whim of the person or force that gave out the suggestion or bent over to do the steering. We could almost see the bend in our friend Walter as he fingered her wheel and pondered on the crassly eyeless character of human appetites.

'It's like a fairy tale,' said Eurona.

'Oh Jesus,' whispered Ben.

*****

That evening Rollo was to make his first attempt at a public address. We were to join him, give him heart and choose a suitable spot. Before we left our Terrace we sought out Morris. We explained to him that Shadrach Sims would dearly love to see Eurona.

'By his tone,' said Walter, 'he's got a very nice job waiting for her. Don't thank us. You are the one who did it really. When Shadrach saw the nimble, two-handed way you took opportunity by the bit after getting that suit which would have sent any other man reeling, he knew that you were the kind of man the Terraces could well use as a homely version of the phoenix, symbol of rebirth, unkillable hope. We agreed but said it was a pity you hadn't managed to double your size as well. That would have been a transformation beyond the scorn of even our bitterest doubters for the way you have shrunk is one of the greatest facts since the last war. We carried on so much about this matter of your size it was only matter of time before Shadrach took out that little book of his again and signed a voucher for a large cloche to cover your head or at least a glass pane in that bowler and a few packages of patent fertiliser to stuff into your shoes for quick results. But we thought of something better. We said the symbol would be complete if the daughter of Morris, a daughter of the shadows as he is their son, could rise with him. So he gave her the clothes. If I were you, Morris, I'd take her down to see him tonight. Strike the Shadrach while he's hot. And give her a chance to speak to him on his own. He has the mind of a poet and he wouldn't like to have you on the outskirts pushing that bowler between him and her.'

'And tell her,' said Ben, 'to use plenty of Fixo.'

'I will, I will.'

We met Rollo at the valley's bed. We walked around some sidestreets looking for one that would be suitable for this raw, young apprentice of fame at our side who was still on the threshold of his public mission. We wanted as much seclusion as possible for Rollo. A place where nobody at all would hear him except ourselves would suit us down to the ground. Had we unleashed him in full hearing of the Terraces the voters would only have to hear the smallest part of his doctrines and they would come bothering us for permission to pull his ears off and there would we be having to tell some of our oldest friends that because Rollo only had two ears many of them would have to be turned away disappointed. As we walked, we flattered Rollo with an almost Moorish unction that seemed to fill the Terraces with mosques, which was a nice change from Christian hovels. We also asked him about Eurona.

'Like a dog,' he said. 'Perfect. She gave me a lot of comfort and calm.'

We found a small, tree-filled corner near a vicarage where there was a pleasant smell of wet leaves and quietude. A great mound of earth had formed around the base of an ancient elm. We invited Rollo to climb on to this mound and explain to the world, us, the Terraces and any voters or dogs that might come around later why equality was a mad myth, adult suffrage a tyranny of the mediocre and rule by Trade Unions as poisoned a cup of cocoa as had ever discoloured the beer-gulping faith of our sounder citizens in Britain and the Empire. Rollo began softly, staring at the drifts of fallen leaves around the tree as if wondering whether some of his audience may not have taken refuge beneath the leaves to keep warm while waiting for the meeting to begin. He could not understand why we were keeping him such a secret. As he spoke, he could see that we were not stirred, that we did not grow to look any less impassive and more than once we saw him writhe with the temptation to turn right around and try his luck with the elm. But it was plain even to Rollo that trees gave less of a damn than we did for the beauties of force as a rule of life, so he stayed right side around. He gradually got a grip on his thoughts and they both rose to the occasion. His voice grew firmer as his ideas grew thinner. We attracted no attention. A few more leaves fell from the branches but we could not put that down directly to Rollo. The vicar poked his head over the vicarage wall and said: 'Well done, my boys. Carry on.' This vicar was short sighted, remiss and kept in well with everybody by making statements of that kind even to groups of militant freethinkers about the Terraces who would sometimes call a meeting to speak angrily about God in some connection or another.

Fifty yards away a man lounged against a wall, undecided about whether or not to come nearer or go further away. Walter knew this man and called him on, eagerly. The man's name was Meirion Mathews. He had the stock face of the Terraces, dark, pensive, limned with wrath. He had several brothers who had been notable for the lives of protest they had lived against the shape and quality of the forces that lay behind the Terraces. His father was a man with bad luck and brittle bones. His legs had been broken so often during his years in the pit, he had been accused by one doctor, young, ignorant and new to the valley and its evils, of spending most of his time underground brooding about revenge and trying to get his own back on the management by kicking sharply at the roof in an attempt to unsettle the workings and treat himself to a new fracture. In this way, even if he could not have the comfort of a disaster, he would at least have another spell in the convalescent home, getting shorter with each fracture, and not minding. In many other ways too the family of Meirion had taken a course in every form of unpleasantness open to the working people. His oldest brother had gone to gaol for obstructing his own eviction and he had been impressed by the much surer footing of tenancy in a State-run institution than in private dwellings, the authorities having been in no hurry to throw him out. Another brother who had a small cottage on the river's bank and a lot of children and little to feed them on save a view of the river's bank, had been washed away ten years before in the great flood that kept the people at the bed of the valley swirling for two or three days. Meirion's brother had not been seen again. Some said he was still alive and had been seen but there was general agreement he had little to come back to and would be wise to remain in any other place that gave him the chance to be dry, fed and untroubled. A younger brother of Meirion had gone out to Spain in the days of the Civil War and had died in the fighting around Madrid. Meirion himself was a slow, patient man. He was not as bright as the remainder of his brothers but he had observed their moments of revolt and their strange, swift vanishing. These things he had stitched into the flag of a private conviction that all was not well among men.

'What's he on about?' he asked Walter.

Walter, not to disturb Rollo who was now giving us an excited summary of a leaflet he had read on German Labour Camps and doing a few free jerks to show us how much saner and springier we would be if we did a term in one of those places, took Meirion to one side.

'Is he one of those Jerkers?' asked Meirion, watching

174

Rollo's quick movements of arm and leg and understanding next to nothing of Rollo's streaming chatter. He was referring to a sect that had blossomed briefly in the Terraces. The people in that sect, impressed as Meirion had been by the rising rhythm of calamity in their midst, had worked out a theory that the evil forces that came sealing up the gushers of joy and beauty in and out of season were like animals, skulking in the failing light of our misfortune and waiting to seize all whose stillness of body betrayed the end of any will to resist. One could keep these animals fooled, skulking and harmless, said the Jerkers, for as long as thirty or forty years, by keeping the limbs in perpetual motion. They had jerked for a month, then gave it up and called for the nearest animal to take note of how quiet they were lying.

'He is no Jerker,' said Walter. 'He is indeed all for those animals in whom the Jerkers believed which wait for our bodies to fall still and ready for the tooth.'

'What's he think is wrong with us?'

'He thinks we're lazy and corrupt.'

'Corrupt? That's bad, isn't it? Isn't that what it means?'

'Rotten. Like the dead. You know about the dead.'

'I've heard about them.'

'That's how we strike Rollo, headstones and all. He also says we breed too much, rob the country of its dignity and drag the Empire to its ruin by our lousy look and servile envy. He wishes to see us given great toil to keep our bodies satisfied and weary. He wishes silence and obedience to be made the great commandments of our lives, to put an end to the evil itch to question and complain in our tongues and minds.'

175

'He wants to do a lot,' said Meirion.

'He's going to be a busy boy, this Rollo.'

Meirion pointed to Rollo's knickers.

'Look at his trousers. They're short.'

'They're supposed to be. They're a new way of covering the legs that Rollo has learned from the rich in whose cause he wishes to strike such blows. But they're only the beginning. Ten more vouchers, bought with the scalps of idle and fertile blokes like you, Meirion, and he gets a short crown to go with them.'

'Is that so?'

They listened again to Rollo, Meirion with his head bent forward in a thoughtful frown. Rollo was now describing the black plagues that had arisen from the scrofulous class spite which the miners and their like had written large upon the banner of their distinct political and industrial organisations. It struck us that Meirion was following the points of Rollo's thesis as he would have followed the dialogue of earth and rain. There was sound, there was feeling. Between them, the desire to express an answer grew slowly, like a plant.

'He's one of them, is he?' asked Meirion.

'Them what?'

'Fascists. The sort our Iestyn went to fight against in Spain?'

'That's it.'

Meirion stepped close to the mound and asked Rollo to bend over. Rollo looked with scorn at Meirion and remained rigid, erect.

'Go on, bend down, Rollo,' said Walter. 'You've made a mark with this Meirion. All he wants is to be sure of the wording of that fine phrase you used about the terrible scrofula of class spite among the poor.'

'He liked it, did he?'

'Why not? Nobody'd know the truth of it better than Meirion. Why, he's got that scrofula so bad he has to have the bits of him stuck back after any attack that's worse than usual. But he's beginning to see the light. After the last attack they stuck him back in the wrong places. So give him a second helping of that splendid metaphor right into the ear.'

Rollo bent over. Meirion's fist came up in a fierce surge of murder that cleared all the sense of mystery from Meirion for a second or two. Ben took a step and caught Rollo on his shoulder as he toppled forward. The smack of Meirion's bone against Rollo's flesh attracted the attention of the vicar. He saw the front of Rollo's face apparently attached to the back of Ben's body. He peered closely but said nothing not wishing to bring forth into the shrinking field of his interest some fresh instance of dark and confusing devilry to stir his dying urge to make sense of the long, unbalanceable account of effort and reward between our hills.

'Well done, my boys,' he said. 'Carry on.'

We took Rollo away. At the bottom of the lane which had been the scene of Rollo's first evangel we soaked a handkerchief in a brook and laid it on his brow. We envied his thoughtless calm as he sat there supine between us. When he showed signs of coming to, we walked him back into the town, still shadowed by the will to doze.

'Ben,' said Walter. 'Call in at the jug section of the Stag and fetch two large flagons of beer for Rollo. He will be weary and sick when he weighs up the fruit of this evening's work. To have an audience of five and tangled ideas is bad enough. To have one of those five hit you rigid before you have the chance of unravelling those ideas is much worse. So get him some beer. It will help him to take a better view of this disorder.'

We reached the back room of the millinery shop. We sat down. Rollo laid his head on the table. We watched him with interest. It was with this very posture that Tudor Phelps had always begun his recitation 'The Last Knell' which showed us Tudor on the point of being taken out and hung. Tudor only had to see a table and he would put his head on it and begin that recitation. Once he got his head back up to the usual level Tudor would tell us fear was filling him with delusions. He would prove this by taking a seat and putting his head down sharply a good yard away from the chair and table and going sprawling. This would show him reason and he would tell us who he was. A peasant whose best crop had always been hemp. It still was. The irony of this strikes Tudor with such bitterness he would laugh up and down an entire octave. He put in so many of these bursts of despairing laughter we lost track of what further thoughts he might be having about fear, life and hemp. At the end he stood up and told us straight that with a conscience like his it would be a pleasure to be hung. We could not see that he was far wide of the mark there. We thought of Tudor and the power of dejection as we sat there and looked at Rollo. He had upon him at that moment the look of absolute defeat that we had come to know so well. We were not without sympathy but it was furtive and without form. We had become so identified with the great new phase of methodical mishaps on this earth that even those who despised us and lived to hurt us, when they too felt the ironic deadly needle that pricks the bubble of wishing and self-illusion, may join our fellowship during the brief moment of their passage outward. But our minds went quickly beyond the shaken aching head of Rollo. We saw the scorn and petty folly of such men corrupting the feeble roots of pity and communion among us, preparing their compost of fermenting lunacies, demanding, to heal the tiny ail of their own bored restlessness, a massive poultice of other men's wretchedness and pain. Knowledge closed the soft forgiving lips of brotherhood.

'That Meirion,' said Arthur, 'grew in good soil. His hatred has a wise integrity. He did all right.'

Ben came in with the beer. We found a glass in a cupboard. We urged Rollo to drink. We took none ourselves. His eyes brightened and he smiled again.

'I'm thinking now,' he said, 'of the miracle that keeps men's faith in themselves and their work intact.'

We put our elbows on the table and thought with him. Being without the beer we did not look as pleased about the miracle as he did.

'Look at me,' he went on. 'I have been without faith this last week. Then that Eurona comes, with her queer white lovely face and gleaming hair. In the humble devotion of her to me my faith finds the food that leads it away from death. The world's daft. I know that. It doesn't deserve one moment of the labour of those leaders who try to improve its ways. But the miracle occurs and the line of pioneers holds firm.'

He drank another glassful and stiffened the miracle some more.

'Tonight again,' he said. 'I will see her and lay the ointment on the sting.'

Ben stood up. I thought he was now going formally to propose that he be allowed to carry on where Meirion left off and reduce Rollo to a state of all sting and one pair of golfing knickers. Before he could speak, the door was thrown open and Morris came dancing in, glowing. He went straight to Walter, not seeing Rollo.

'We're there,' he shouted. 'There at last. It was just like you said, Walter. You're a wizard, boy. That's why I came along here now. I remembered you said you sometimes came to the back of this shop in the nights and I wanted you to be the first to know. I took Eurona down to Shadrach like you said. He was taken with her from the start what with the yellow and the Fixo and her eyes gleaming and me bowing and scraping and being pleasant and all. I left her there with him in his room, under that lamp. Good God, have you seen that lamp? There's a lamp. Shadrach looked full of it. If me and Eurona don't land a couple of cosy little jobs out of this from Shadrach my new suit isn't purple and my name isn't Morris.'

There was a violent sound of smashing glass. We looked at Rollo. He had hurled the drinking glass against the wall. He stood up. His nostrils were dilated, stiff as board, as if they had drawn the firmness from his mouth which had become slack, shapeless. Now he looked like Tudor Phelps' very twin. He left the room, clutching a flagon. Morris was puzzled and afraid. He ran to Rollo, looked up at him

180

wondering and then ran back to us like a hunting dog. He asked Walter to do something. Walter quickened his step and came abreast of Rollo.

'Always,' said Walter in a low clear voice to Rollo. 'Always between the young and the strong and the glory which they seek stand the old and cunning merchants, the men of wealth who live only for as long as the weak and stupid lie down to make a pasture for their greed, the cunning men who take you up and squeeze you for their use, then lay you in the closet. Men like Sims. After him, boy.'

'What do you think this Rollo is up to?' Morris asked us who were following, looking at Arthur.

'Perhaps he is going to give Shadrach a drink,' said Arthur.

Morris giggled on hearing that, relieved. He ran ahead and crouched to take a look at the bottle in Rollo's hand. He let his jaw drop and ran back to us.

'But it's empty,' he said.

'Then he's going to lay it across Shad's head.'

'Hard, you mean?'

'As hard as he can, no doubt.'

'Good God!' said Morris, going above our heads.

We thought Morris would start shouting for help at this point. But we were already at the foot of the stairs that led to the apartment of Shadrach. Rollo climbed them firmly, making, we thought, more noise than he needed to make and clanging the bottle against the wall of the stairway to make the universe less full of himself. He opened the door of Shadrach's room. The divan and the lamp were as they had

181

been before. Shadrach was there, standing by the divan, red faced, masterful and suave. He wore a brown velvet jacket that spoke straightaway of autumn to our sorrow-seeking eyes. He was looking down at Eurona who was staring up at him as amazed and accepting as a girl of her weight could be. She was, judging by her look, in the fullest sense, on her way out of the pigeon's cot, her longings on the wing and about to be handled by as smooth-fingered a fancier as these Terraces would ever see. The evening was an astonishing reversal of everything that Eurona had ever known and as the syllables of her grey catechism of shyness and restraint gibbered their way out of sight and meaning, her tiny disciplines whirled like Katherine wheels in the wreck. If we ever become interested in love as a sport we shall use that scene as a text book. We shall have a lamp with just that degree of brilliance, a divan with just that depth of spring, a length of brown velvet enough to make a jacket down to the feet and autumnal to the point of driving the birds southwards every time we come into sight. The whole background looked fetching to us and must have been a beacon to the senses of any maiden whose fingers have been coarsened by sack matting and kitchen ashes to within an inch of the line where the gift of ecstasy dips down and dies.

Rollo rushed in to the attack. Shadrach ran to meet him. We had known in advance that neither of these two would dawdle in a situation like that. Rollo laid the bottle over Shadrach's head as if he had no further use for either the bottle or the head. Morris sprang into action on his own account, gripped Rollo by the legs and pitched him over with an agility which may have been helped by a bite at

Rollo's golf stocking and the leg beneath. Rollo's head hit the floor hard and he lay there as quietly as Shadrach himself. It was good to see two such dynamic characters lying there looking so still and tolerant. Morris fell on his knees beside Shadrach, ran his fingers over his brow and called on him to awake, awake. Eurona stood for a few seconds, undecided. She looked pityingly at Rollo and we expected to see her getting down beside him and doing as much stroking for him as her father was doing for Shadrach. She decided that if stroking were to be done on the brow of a man who would not be immediately the wiser for this stroking it had better be done on the brow of Shadrach who had a way of speaking to her that made her feel at ease in the world and whose gratitude would bring a brighter beam on the day of need. She got down and shared Shadrach's head with her father. Rollo lay there looking neglected as well as senseless. If he could have realised the full meaning of his condition, he would have said about being stunned what Tudor Phelps in that recitation had said about being hung. That it was a pleasure, thank you. For thirty seconds we watched this cameo. Then we went to inform whatever branch of the Government looks after people who are on the floor without any wish to be there.

*****

So there we were. Shadrach went back to complete his meditation and frolic in that mansion, his hatred of the valley septic, insoluble, not to be endured. Rollo went to the

183

County Prison for a short spell of brooding on his destiny, edging nearer to whatever end will be arranged for him by the nerves within and the men and things without. Eurona, at the pressing request of her father and the Government, went to do her duty at the home of that foxhunter. Morris slipped back into his mood of quiet submission, viewing and making deep obeisance before his purple suit on days of feast and commemoration. And we, for another interlude, went back to our wall, to trace the circular, intricate thoughts that came to us as the downsag of our half-baked being found comfort in the hard, shrewd upthrust of well-baked brick.

LIBRARY of WALES
FUNDED BY

Llywodraeth Cynulliad Cymru
Welsh Assembly Government

**CYNGOR LLYFRAU CYMRU
WELSH BOOKS COUNCIL**

LIBRARY OF WALES

The Library of Wales is a Welsh Assembly Government project designed to ensure that all of the rich and extensive literature of Wales which has been written in English will now be made available to readers in and beyond Wales. Sustaining this wider literary heritage is understood by the Welsh Assembly Government to be a key component in creating and disseminating an ongoing sense of modern Welsh culture and history for the future Wales which is now emerging from contemporary society. Through these texts, until now unavailable, out-of-print or merely forgotten, the Library of Wales brings back into play the voices and actions of the human experience that has made us, in all our complexity, a Welsh people.

The Library of Wales includes prose as well as poetry, essays as well as fiction, anthologies as well as memoirs, drama as well as journalism. It will complement the names and texts that are already in the public domain and seek to include the best of Welsh writing in English, as well as to showcase what has been unjustly neglected. No boundaries will limit the ambition of the Library of Wales to open up the borders that have denied some of our best writers a presence in a future Wales. The Library of Wales has been created with that Wales in mind: a young country not afraid to remember what it might yet become.

Dai Smith
Raymond Williams Chair in the Cultural History of Wales,
Swansea University

Foreword by Ian Rowlands

Ian Rowlands is a playwright and director whose work has been at the forefront of Welsh drama in English and Welsh since the emergence of his first plays in the 1990s. Born in the Terraces, he caught a bus out of the valley at an early age to train at the Welsh College of Music and Drama. He has been the artistic director of several Welsh theatre companies and has written extensively for tv, theatre and radio. His most notable plays include the multi-award winning *Marriage of Convenience*, *Butterfly* and *Blink*.

Though he now lives in Carmarthen, the Terraces of his youth remain dear to his heart.

Cover image by John Elwyn

Born near Newcastle Emlyn in 1916, John Elwyn's work vividly explores the hills, fields, buildings and people of rural west Wales – the south Cardiganshire countryside of his childhood.

A student of the Royal College of Art, Elwyn was recognised as a fine figure painter. He also depicted the industrial land-scapes and mining communities of south Wales as well as painting contemporary Welsh writers and friends including Glyn Jones and Leslie Norris. John Elwyn died in 1997.

LIBRARY OF WALES SERIES EDITOR: DAI SMITH

'This landmark series is testimony to the resurgence of the English-language literature of Wales. After years of neglect, the future for Welsh writing in English – both classics and new writing – looks very promising indeed.'

M. Wynn Thomas

WWW.LIBRARYOFWALES.ORG

LIBRARY OF WALES
titles are available to buy online at:

gwales.com
Llyfrau ar-lein
Books on-line